Tug Lake Tales

BARBARA J. KING

Copyright © 2016 Barbara J. King
All rights reserved.
ISBN: 153547162X
ISBN-13: 978-1535471626

Dedication and Thanks

I dedicate this book to my wonderful husband, Roger, and my loving and supportive family. I also dedicate this book to all of those who taught in one room country schoolhouses.

Thank you to Lee Pulaski and Terry Misfeldt for editing and proofreading *Tug Lake Tales*. Also, a word of thanks to the members of the Shawano Area Writers for their encouragement and suggestions. Without you, this novel would still be in a desk drawer.

Foreword

Tug Lake Tales is a collection of stories based on my recollections as a little girl attending a one room country school during the fifties and sixties, plus the memories of forty-two years of elementary school teaching. The description of the school, the games we played at recess and the programs we performed for our parents are as close as I can remember.

This work is fiction. Some of the events did take place, but not exactly as described. There are also things that could have taken place, but didn't, so my imagination took over.

My characters are not based on one real person, but combinations of children I went to school with and students I have taught. The names of the characters were popular names at that time and not necessarily the name of anyone I knew.

Hop on the school bus and let's head for Tug Lake School, thirteen miles outside of Merrill in the northwoods of Wisconsin in the mid-twentieth century for a school year of fun and learning.

Chapter One
The First Day

"Wow! Yippee! Yahoo!" was how I felt as I stopped on the bus steps to gaze at Tug Lake School! My first day of school! It's no exaggeration to say that I had waited my entire life, all six years of it, for this exact moment! I could ride the bus and go to school with my brother and sister! I couldn't wait to learn to read and write! I could go home tonight and read all my books by myself!

"For crying out loud, Jean, move!" My big sister, Susan, put her hand in the middle of my back and pushed me down the bus steps. "If you were any slower, you'd be a turtle!"

"And if you were any uglier, you'd be mud!" I yelled back.

Susan headed up the grassy hill to the front porch where a group of eighth-grade girls were talking, not bothering to use the rutted path the teacher used to drive her car closer to the school.

I stopped again to really look at the school, my school, for the next eight years.

Tug Lake School didn't look like those little red schoolhouses that you think of when someone says "one-room country schoolhouse" or the big brick schools in Merrill. No, indeed, it was a huge white rectangular wooden structure with a covered open porch running across the front with a belfry that had a big brass bell peeking out. It stood on the top of a grassy hill with teeter-totters and swings in the back and a big sand lot below the hill where a bigger boy was already by the backstop hitting balls to some other boys with gloves. A tall wire fence went all the way around the school. I thought it was beautiful.

"Jeannie, get out of the way! The bus is turning around." Billy, my older brother by about five years, grabbed my arm and dragged me out of the path of the approaching yellow bus. The bus had let us off at the bottom of the hill.

"Billy, hurry up! Let's play some Batter's Up before the bell rings." one of his friends yelled as he ran past Billy to the field.

"Why don't you play on the merry-go-round?" Billy pointed me in the right direction and ran off to meet his friends on the ball field.

I walked through the dewy, wet grass, trying to avoid getting grass stains on my new saddle shoes. I passed a small group of boys discussing the teacher's new turquoise Desoto. Boys sure like cars. I don't get it.

I stopped to give my anklets, which were slowly sliding down into my shoes, a tug, which meant I had to sit my new red plaid book bag in the wet grass to give my socks a two-handed tug.

Halfway up the hill stood the merry-go-round jammed with kids of all sizes and ages. Two older boys were standing in the rut worn around the merry-go-round and pushing the bars to make it go faster to the screams of the girls.

Some boys were trying to jump on by grabbing the metal bars as it spun past. Once in a while, someone would grab a bar and hang on long enough to be pulled to safety, but mostly they would miss entirely and fall on their face in the worn rut. They'd get up off the ground, sheepishly wiping off their pants while everyone hooted and hollered.

I stood by a couple of girls about my age. I knew them because they had older brothers and sisters in my mother's 4-H club and would come along so we could play.

Someone shouted, "Hey, let the little girls get on!"

There was a great deal of feet dragging and holding on to the bars before the machine squealed to a halt.

We just stood there.

"You're not too chicken to get on, are you?" an older boy taunted.

All at once, we girls scrambled to get on. I was so short, I had trouble pulling myself onto the slippery red painted boards. Desperately, I clambered to find a bar to hold on to. The merry-go-round slowly started to spin and I could feel myself sliding to the edge. I was still clutching my beautiful new, red plaid shiny dinner pail, I had to make a decision and make it quickly. Either I let go of the dinner pail and grab the bar, or I hold on to it and fly off. I let go of the dinner pail and grabbed the bar. I saw a blur of red as my beautiful dinner pail rolled over and over in the grass.

"Here. I'll help you." A big boy grabbed my shoulder and pulled me safely away from the edge. My dress caught on the rough boards on the edge of the merry-go-round as I scooted back. I heard a ripping sound. There, near the hem of the skirt was a big ugly tear. I was wearing my favorite dress, the blue plaid one with the white collar and three white buttons on the top and now it had a big rip, but this wasn't the time to worry about it. I had my hands full just trying to stand up, hang on and squeal with the rest of the girls, as we sped around faster and faster. I loveeed school!

Just as someone yelled, "I'm gonna throw up!" the school bell in the belfry started striking loudly.

There was a great effort to slow the merry-go round with all the long-legged kids sitting down and dragging their feet. I was about to jump off when an older girl in green pushed me hard and I landed on my face in the dirt.

"Clumsy." The girl in green with a long brown ponytail, about Billy's age, smirked at me as she swished past me with her million can-can petticoats. She walked over to two other girls with equally puffy skirts. One had beautiful coppery hair down to her waist and a ton of freckles on her face and arms. The other had short permed hair and brown glasses which had slid down to the edge of her nose, making her eyes appear big and owl-like.

The girl in green said something to her friends. They all looked at me and laughed before turning to line up for school. I was so mad. I pounded my fist in the dirt.

"Here, Squirt." Billy reached down and pulled me to my feet. "What happened?"

"That girl in the green dress pushed me off the merry-go-round." I looked down to see a thin trickle of blood making its way down my dusty knee and legs.

"Yeah, that's Karla. She's a mean one. She picks on everyone. The pretty one is her cousin, Marian and the other one is Donna. Here." He pushed a clean hanky into my hands. It smelled so good, of home and Oxydol laundry soap. I managed to stop the bleeding and wipe the majority of dust and dirt from my dress and my body.

Billy came up the hill shaking my Thermos bottle. I could hear something rattling around inside.

"You broke the glass liner in your Thermos bottle. We'll have to throw the whole thing out. You can't drink glass and it won't keep your milk cold anyway."

Tears filled my eyes and Billy put his arm around me. "It's okay, Squirt, you can have my milk and Thermos bottle. I don't drink it anyway." I knew that was a lie but, a sweet lie. "I'm afraid your dinner pail isn't too good either." My beautiful red plaid dinner pail had a big dent in one corner and a couple smaller ones.

As we trudged up the hill to join the other kids at the flag pole, I heard. "Billy, your little sister sure is a mess. Didn't anyone tell her not to wear her barn clothes to school? I can smell her from here," Karla pinched her nose closed with two fingers. The redhead grinned at me and "owl girl" giggled right out loud.

"Karla, didn't anyone ever tell you, you're ugly and you have a big mouth!" Billy shouted.

"Ooooo!" Karla squealed before singing in a whiny, irritating voice,

"Sticks and stones will break my bones
But words will never hurt me."

"Hey, where do you think you're going?" Billy grabbed my arm.

"To see if a kick in the rear will hurt her."

"Hold on, little sister, or you'll be kicked out of school before you ever get in the building."

"I can't let her get away with that!"

"Don't worry, Squirt. She'll get hers. Bullies always do. You have to ignore her."

I didn't know what he was talking about, so I just nodded.

He stared at me and a big grin reached his dark chocolate brown eyes, half hidden by the unruly black hair that kept falling over his forehead. "You are kind of a mess."

"I tore my new dress, too," I said, showing him the rip.

"Don't worry. Maybe if you're nice to Susan, she'll sew it before Mom sees it."

"I don't think so. I already told Susan that she's as ugly as dirt."

"You've been pretty busy!" Billy exclaimed as he tugged at one of my blonde permed curls. We joined the other kids already encircling the flagpole. Susan gave me a big sister disapproving look when she saw me. I pretended not to notice.

Two eighth grade boys attached the huge flag to the rope on the flagpole and raised it as everyone said the Pledge of Allegiance. Except I didn't, because I didn't know it.

"I pledge allegiance to the Flag of the United States of America and to the Republic for which it stands, one nation, indivisible, with liberty and justice for all."

We then filed into the school into a dark, narrow hallway where the boys hung their coats and everyone stored their dinner pails on a high long shelf. Billy helped me put mine on the shelf.

"What happened to you?" Susan whispered to me as she placed her lunch box beside mine on the shelf. I just shrugged. I didn't need Susan scolding me right now, besides my stomach was filled with butterflies.

She whispered, "Follow me," and gave my hand a squeeze.

The girls' coatroom was another long hallway at the other end of the school. It was painted yellow and the morning sun coming through the window at the end made everything look bright and pretty. Everyone quickly claimed a hook and I was left with the one behind the door.

The teacher poked her head in the door, telling us to hurry. It was time to pick desks.

After peeling myself off the wall, I followed the other girls into the classroom. It was a huge white rectangular room with blackboards the full length of the front and back walls. One wall had tall windows that reached up to the ceiling. On the other wall was an open area that had a load of books, the library, and four doors. I later learned the four doors were a kitchen, with a stove and sink, where we washed our hands for lunch, the boy and girls' coatrooms and a storage room we called the teacher's room. An old wooden upright piano was pushed against the wall between the teacher's room and the girls' hall. There was a shiny white bubbler by the boys' hallway door. I couldn't wait to take a drink. The room smelled like good things such as floor wax, furniture polish, books, crayons, and paints.

Everyone was milling around. Teacher was calling all thirty-six students by grades to choose their desks. Eighth grade got to pick first, because they had been there the longest and had the right to first choice. I knew Susan, of course, and her friends Arlene, Dorothy, and Carol because they had been to the house. Then there was the tallest boy I ever saw named Leroy. The last boy was Tom who had a brother named John in my grade. Susan chose a desk between two of her friends, Dorothy and Carol.

The seventh grade had Karla and Donna, who unfortunately I had already met, Billy, Junior and Ray. When it was Billy's turn he sat between a pretty girl named Arlene and his best friend Ray.

The sixth grade had the pretty girl, Marian, a large girl, Sheila, and Lois, who hadn't said a word to anyone. There were only two boys in that class, Frank, who must have thought he was Frankie Avalon, the way he combed his hair and held it in place with Brylecreem, and Andy, who was always fooling around.

Fifth grade was mostly boys: Gary; Jimmy, who was really fat; Jake, Frank's brother, who fixed his hair the same way as Frank; and Andy. The only girl was Diane. I knew her from 4-H. She was really good at sports.

Fourth grade had Fred; Darlene, Marian's sister; Peggy, Sheila's sister, and they had a younger sister Cheryl in second grade, and a cute boy named Keith.

Third grade had two girls, Judy and Carlene and twins Matthew and Mark.

In second grade was Sandy, Gary's sister, David, Cheryl, and James.

Since my class was just starting, we had no rights and got the leftovers. Luckily, when everyone had chosen, there were four small desks left, just enough. My classmates were Roger, John, and a pretty girl named Cora.

The desks were great! They were made out of wood with a metal frame and a seat attached. The top lifted up and there was a little metal pencil holder in the front where I stored my yellow pencils and big green eraser that smelled like potato chips when you rubbed it. Next was a wooden ruler, silver scissors and a wide ruled writing tablet with a big red cover and the picture of an Indian chief on it. It had Big Chief Tablet written in black letters at the top.

I finished putting away my school supplies just in time. Teacher had an announcement. She was no longer Miss Kleinschmidt. Instead, she was Mrs. Webb. She had gotten married over the summer vacation. Susan, Dorothy and Carol nodded knowingly at each other. Karla and her friends batted their eyelashes and giggled. Older girls act so silly when you mention marriage. I was thrilled because I didn't have to say Kleinschmidt all the time and it was about time she got married. She was really getting old, almost thirty!

Mrs. Webb was really pretty. I'm sure she looked a lot like Mrs. Claus in her younger days. She had a round cheery face with pink cheeks, sparkling blue eyes, reddish-brown curly hair and a chubby little body. She never raised her voice, but everyone paid attention and did what she wanted, even dumb old Karla and her friends.

One class at a time, Mrs. Webb called up each of the seven other grades. She handed them reading textbooks with tons of pages and lots of colored pictures and told them to read the first story and answer the questions on a sheet with purple letters. I could hardly wait until it was our turn.

When it was our time, we sat at the table and stuck out our hands, but instead of getting a book, teacher pointed with a skinny stick to a long strip of paper on the blackboard. She explained this was the alphabet and there were twenty-six letters, each letter had its own sound and sometimes two. When we knew all the letters and sounds we could make words and books were stories made of words. Who knew?

Mrs. Webb gave Roger, John, Cora and I each a cardboard capital "A" and a small "a." We traced the letters with our pointer finger saying the long "a" sound like in ape. Then we traced the letters saying the short "a" sound like in apple. We did this for a long time. Then teacher gave us a plain sheet of paper and told us to fill the paper with capital and small "a's" by tracing the cardboard letters with a pencil. This was kind of tricky because the pencil kept going too wide or sliding onto the cardboard. When we finished, teacher looked at all our papers.

"Very nice, John," Mrs. Webb said, placing a big gold sticky star on his paper. John had straight rows of capital and small "a's" on his paper. The rest of us had shaky ghost letters all over our page. She taped John's paper to the chalkboard and said that the rest of us got to keep ours to show our family.

"I'm glad my paper wasn't hung on the chalkboard," Cora whispered. "I want to take mine home to show my mother."

"Me, too," I whispered, looking at my messy paper. I guess Cora wanted her paper hung up with a gold sticky star as much as I did.

Then each first grader was given a box of eight fat crayons and a paper full of little purple outlined pictures to color.

"Phew, this stinks," Roger exclaimed, sniffing his paper. Of course, we all had to smell our papers too. It smelled like rubbing alcohol.

"That's the ink I use in the mimeograph machine which runs off your worksheet copies."

We all stared at Mrs. Webb having no idea what she was talking about.

Mrs. Webb lead us to the workroom, where there stood a big gray machine on a metal stand. She took a paper with raised purple letters, stuck it in a slot face up and starting turning the handle. Paper after paper came out looking just like the first one. We each got a chance to turn the handle. I love modern things!

Then we were sent back to our desks and spent the rest of the reading time making letters and coloring long "a" and short "a" pictures. This whole reading thing might take a whole lot longer than I had first thought. That was all right. I was going to be at Tug Lake School for eight years.

Chapter Two
Field Trip

"Yuck! You're eating paste!" I exclaimed.

"No, I'm not," Roger denied.

"You are, too," Cora piped up. "There's some on your lip."

The first graders were at the back table busily coloring, cutting and pasting pictures of things that started with the letter "s." I had just pasted a green snake next to a yellow sun when I saw Roger eating the paste.

"Try it, it's good," Roger stuck his hand back in the big plastic jar of Lepage paste and took his time licking the sticky glob off his fingers.

"You'll get your guts all stuck together," Cora insisted.

"Doesn't your mother feed you breakfast?" I laughed.

"I don't live with my mother," he whispered. "I live with my foster parents."

I hadn't expected that answer. Imagine, not living with your own mother and dad! I didn't expect the sad look on his long, thin face either, but I pushed on. "Don't they feed you?"

"Sure, but this is good. Try it."

Cora and I each made a face, but John stuck his hand in the jar and started licking his fingers.

"Not bad."

"See, I told you," Roger insisted.

Cora and I looked at each other and yelled, "Mrs. Webb, Roger and John are eating paste!"

"Roger! John!" she exclaimed. "Here, this will taste better." She reached into a desk drawer, pulled out two graham crackers and gave one to Roger and one to John.

"Mrs. Webb, we're eating paste, too," Cora and I chorused. She laughed and produced two more crackers.

We had finished our pasting and were sent back to our seat to practice writing the letters we had already learned.

Ouch! I felt something on my neck. As the cold weather started coming, the horseflies came inside. Those pesky horseflies were big and didn't just land on a person like regular houseflies. They bit. Mrs. Webb had hung up flypaper. Not only was it disgusting looking with all the dead bugs glued to it, it didn't help that much anymore. I waved my hand around to discourage any pests.

Ping! Ping! Ping! I felt three more stings, on my arm, my forehead and my cheek. These weren't horseflies! Ping! Something hit my nose and then something landed in my hair. I untangled a pink piece of broken eraser from my hair. Ping! Ping! Ping! They were coming fast and furious now! Some were hitting me, but most were bouncing off my desk and landing on the floor. I looked around and there was Roger with a little pile of broken eraser bits sitting on his half-finished paper. He flicked another at me, then grinned an evil grin as he prepared to bombard me some more.

Before I could raise my hand and tell the teacher, we heard, "Roger." The stern tone startled both of us.

Ah ha, I thought. *Now he'll get it.*

Instead, Mrs. Webb said, "Roger, it's time to turn on the radio."

Roger unwound his skinny legs from around the legs of the desk and marched like a soldier to the front of the room. Every week, it was Roger's job to turn on the radio for our weekly music class from the Wisconsin Public Radio station. He'd pass out the booklets of songs and then sit by the brown Philco radio during the program.

> *"Sing your way home at the close of the day*
> *Sing your way home chase the shadows away..."*

As the strains of the theme song filled the air, Mrs. Webb gathered what was left of Roger's little ammunition pile and whispered to me to clean up the mess around my desk. As I picked up the little bits of eraser, I stuck my tongue out at Roger when the teacher wasn't looking. It was totally lost on him. Roger was sitting with the radio blaring in his ear, eyes scrunched shut, head thrown back, singing his heart out at the top of his lungs.

At recess, Cora and I followed John and Roger and a bunch of other boys to a place in the back of the school where a big circle had been worn in the dirt from many years of playing marbles.

Roger was good at the game. He had a leather pouch full of colorful marbles he had won from other players plus two shooters, a bright blue one and a metal one called a steely. Roger was doing great. He looked up to see Gary, a fourth grader, watching the others with his fists shoved in the same worn patched pants he wore to school every day. There were lots of kids in Gary's family, so Gary's clothes had been worn by five others and were pretty raggedy looking by the time they got to him. Gary, standing off to the side, looked wistfully at the other boys.

"Gary, come play," Roger called to him. "I'll make room." Roger shoved over.

"Hey, watch what you're doing! I was about to shoot." Thomas jabbed Roger in the arm with his elbow.

"Come on. Nobody else can beat me today."

Gary shrugged, "Can't, lost my shooter."

"How'd you do that?"

Gary reached into one of the pockets and drew out the lining. Gary didn't have a pouch, so he kept all his marbles in his pants pockets. In the corner of the pocket was a big hole.

"Are you sure it's not with your other marbles?" Roger looked at the bulging pocket on the other side.

"Nope, already looked."

Roger opened his marble pouch and dug around. Finally, he reached out his hand to Gary. Lying in his palm was a large metal shooter. "Here, you can have this."

Gary put his hands behind him. "I can't take your lucky steely. You said you'd keep it 'til the end of the world!"

"It was the end of the world for you." Roger tossed the steely to Gary. "Get playing, recess is almost over, we don't have time to waste!"

* * *

That afternoon, Mrs. Webb announced that we were going on a field trip.

"What's a field trip?" I asked Roger.

"I guess it's where everyone takes a trip to a field."

Roger wasn't too far off with his guess. We were each to pick a partner and go across the road to the woods. We were to collect different kinds of leaves and identify them. The first graders only had to identify five, the older kids twenty.

Mrs. Webb held up two different pictures. Those were the two kinds of poison ivy. One picture showed a low bushy plant with leaves in clusters of three. The other kind was a vine that grew up fence posts and trees.

Nobody had to tell me about poison ivy. Susan got poison ivy every year, even if she didn't go near it. One year, it was all over her body, a red rash with leaky white pimples. It had itched so bad she had taken baths two or three times a day in oatmeal. She had to wear mittens taped to her hands so she wouldn't scratch it at night. Her body was stained pink from calamine lotion. I had never gotten poison ivy and sure didn't want it!

We were to stay close to the path, an old logging road, as much as possible, so no one would get lost. We picked partners. The girls held hands but the boys were trying to shove each other off the trail into the woods. Soon, no one was holding hands. Everyone was running around the edge of the woods finding leaves. Soon, Cora and I each had five different good-looking leaves, not a rip or a tear on them. We found a log to sit on under an oak tree and played tea party with the acorn shells. We soon got bored and started playing hide-and-seek. There were so many good places to hide.

"I gotta go to the bathroom," Cora said as she was dancing around.

"Where?"

"Here's some brush I can hide behind. You be my lookout."

I wasn't a very good lookout. I found a nest that had four blue broken shells in it. It had fallen to the ground, and I was looking for another bush to put it in.

"What do I use for toilet paper?" Cora yelled.

"Grass or leaves, I guess."

"Here's some pretty shiny ones, I'll use those."

When Cora was finished, we decided we better get back to the rest of the school. We looked around for the rest of the kids, but they were nowhere to be seen.

"Where did we come from?" I asked.

"Over there." We both said at once and pointed in opposite directions. It was starting to get darker in the woods and things looked differently.

"If we get to the path, they'll find us."

Cora started off in a direction that was halfway between the two directions we had pointed. I came shuffling behind her, staying close, but trying not to step on her heels. After about what we thought was two hours of stumbling over logs and through branches we heard voices shouting, "Jean! Cora!"

"Help! Help! We're here!" we yelled back.

"They're here!" somebody shouted and kids came crashing through the brush and from behind the trees. Susan and Billy both gave me a hug, then Susan started scolding me about leaving the trail. Luckily, Mrs. Webb came puffing up and gave both Cora and I a big hug, interrupting Susan.

"Girls, for goodness sake! I told you not to wander off. You could have gotten hurt."

"I had to pee," Cora whimpered.

"You should have let me know. It's a good thing Roger remembered where he last saw you, so you were only missing about ten minutes."

I turned to thank our hero and saw him hiding behind a tree poking Peggy in the back with a long branch. Every time she turned to see who was jabbing her, he ducked back behind the tree. He looked busy. I guess the thanks could wait.

* * *

It was a blustery fall day. The wind was ripping the few remaining leaves off the trees and whipping the sand on the baseball field into mini-tornadoes. Roger and I had been gathering sticks and leaves for a fort some of us were building. We had been behind the school when the bell rang. By the time we reached the front door, everyone else had gone inside. I grabbed the cold brass handle of the big wooden door and pulled. It opened a little bit only to bang shut again. This happened three times. The force of the wind lashing through the open porch was so strong, I couldn't open the bulky door.

"Here, let me try," Roger grabbed the handle but didn't have any better luck than I had.

"Let's both pull," Roger suggested.

On the count of three, we both braced our feet on the floor and pulled with all our might. The door opened about a foot when a strong gust of wind whipped through the porch wrenching the heavy door from our grasp and slamming it into the big kitchen window. The glass shattered with a terrifying sound and fell like rain around Roger and me. We froze where we were, too shocked to move. All the kids, followed by Mrs. Webb, came rushing out. They gasped when they saw the mess.

"You're in trouble now, squirty squirt," Karla whispered in my ear. Tears started pouring down my face and my nose got all runny. Someone shoved a hanky in my hands. It was Susan, who had her arm around my shoulder. Billy looked like he was ready to punch anyone who said something nasty to me. I wish he would have heard Karla.

"What happened?" Mrs. Webb asked in a kindly voice.

"I was trying to open the door..." Roger explained how it happened, leaving out my part of the disaster. I stared at him. I couldn't let him take the blame for me too. What if his foster parents decided he was too much trouble and sent him away? It would be all my fault because I let him take all the blame.

"Mrs. Webb, it wasn't all Roger's fault," I confessed. "I was helping him pull the door open because we weren't strong enough to do it alone with the wind pushing it." I might get in trouble, but my conscience felt a whole lot better.

Neither Roger or I got in trouble. Mrs. Webb merely said, "Accidents happen." She gave Karla and her group the look only teachers and mothers have and nobody said anything else. The eighth grade boys found some cardboard and boarded up the window.

My mother just hugged me when she heard and my dad offered to pay for the new window. Roger was not sent away and his foster parents paid for half the window.

When the bus dropped us off at school Monday, we were all surprised. The beautiful front porch had been replaced by a shed-like entryway.

Karla and her group made a big deal about how ugly it was and were about to pick on Roger and me when Billy said, "That was a dumb thing to have a heavy door right by a window anyhow. Let's play ball." And they did.

Chapter Three
My Best Friend

"Where have you been?" I anxiously asked Cora as she climbed off the bus. Cora had patches of redness on her skin, even scabs on her face and arms.

"Did you have chicken pox? You've been gone a week."

"I had poison ivy, and it's all your fault!"

"How can you getting poison ivy be my fault?"

"Remember when we went on the field trip and got lost?"

How could I forget? Susan tattled at home and Daddy sat me down in his office and lectured me for over an hour about following directions and safety in the woods. I now know how to find north by finding moss on a tree, covering up with leaves and grass at night to stay warm and a ton of other things that I hope I never have to use.

"Remember, I had to pee and there wasn't any toilet paper? You told me to use leaves and it was poison ivy."

"You're kidding! I didn't tell you to use poison ivy, for goodness sake. After Mrs. Webb showed us pictures of poison ivy, I thought you'd have brains enough to know what it looked like."

That's the trouble with Cora. She thinks she's never to blame for anything. No matter what goes wrong, it's not her fault. She is the stubbornest, most pig-headed person you've ever met and my best friend in the whole world.

"Are you calling me dumb because I got poison ivy?" Cora demanded, putting her hands on her hips and looking me straight in the eye.

"No," I said putting my hands on my hips and staring straight back. "I'm saying you're dumb for using poison ivy as toilet paper after just seeing a picture of it."

Cora frowned and looked like she was going to cry, so I knew I had better do something to patch things up.

"Of course, those pictures never look like the real thing, anyway, and I probably would have done the same thing." I wouldn't have done that in a million years, but Cora likes to think that she isn't alone when she does stupid stuff.

Cora has two older sisters with kids of their own and a sister in high school. Cora's the baby of the family, like me, but Cora's mother spoils her rotten. She always has the nicest dresses and shoes and wears big floppy bows in her naturally curly blonde hair and all the boys like her, but she's not sissy. She can climb trees as good as the boys and the bow only stays in her hair until her mother can't see her, then she stuffs it in her book-bag.

She's not even afraid of snakes. Cora has every toy she ever wanted, but she's not selfish or snobbish like Karla and her friends and never makes fun of poor kids and always thinks of fun things to do.

"What happened to the porch?" Cora stopped so fast, I ran into her. I told her the whole story and she gave me a big hug. "Let's go play jacks."

That's another good thing about Cora; she never stays mad long.

Cora loves to play jacks. Cora is the best jacks player in the whole school. She has really big hands with extremely long fingers. Her mother calls them pianist hands, which is dumb, because Cora never played the piano in her life, but those hands were just made for playing jacks. Cora can hold ten jacks and a ball in one hand and still have room left over.

Maybe it was because Cora still had scabs on her right hand, but when the bell rang to line up for the Pledge, I was at foursies and she was only at twosies.

Cora quickly gathered her jacks and called back to me, "Come on, pokey."

I yelled, "Wait for me!" She didn't. She's such a poor sport. That's why it's so much fun when I do beat her. I managed to sneak in beside Sandy just as they started the Pledge.

Sandy is in second grade and one of Gary's sisters. She's really quiet until you get to know her. She's the middle child in her family of eleven. Her clothes seldom match and are either too small or too big, but she's nice and fun to play with. Sandy isn't good in reading, so Mrs. Webb put her in our reading group. Even though it's her second time with these stories, she still has trouble. Mrs. Webb let Cora and I practice with her out in the girls' hallway.

Our reading class was always the last to be called, so Cora and I were practicing with Sandy when Cora came up with the idea of playing hide-and-seek in the basement. After all: "Go, Jane, go," "Run, Dick, run," and "See Spot run" isn't all that interesting!

"What if Mrs. Webb comes looking for us?" I asked.

"She won't and if she does we'll say we were going to the bathroom." Cora started tiptoeing down the stairs. Of course, Sandy and I were right behind her.

The basement was a big empty room that went the full length of the school, except for the furnace room, the boys" and girls' bathrooms were at opposite ends and a stack of desks piled up in the far corner. We had modern bathrooms, not an outhouse like some schools. In each bathroom was a hole cut in the floor with a toilet placed over it. There was no way to flush it, so teacher poured stuff in it every day so it wouldn't stink. We had a sink with running water and a small, cloudy mirror on the wall.

"I'll be first. You two go hide. Just don't scream if someone touches you in the dark." Cora leaned face first against the cement wall and started counting to fifty.

It was so dark, I couldn't see a thing. I started in the direction of the furnace room. My eyes adjusted to the dark and I hurried to hide behind the furnace. I heard something behind me. I turned and was nose to nose with Sandy. We both stifled a scream and jumped.

"Why don't you go somewhere else?" I scolded in a whisper trying to cover up my fear.

"I'm too scared," she whispered back and grabbed my arm.

"You're it!" Cora squealed as she jabbed us in the back. She had sneaked up behind us.

Sandy and I screamed at the top of our lungs. We heard chairs being pushed back, running feet and the door opening to the girls' hallway. We just managed to get to the bottom of the stairs when the whole school came rushing down. Mrs. Webb was the last down the steps.

"What's the matter?"

"What's wrong?"

"Are you all right?"

"What's going on?"

Everyone was talking at once. Sandy and I just stood there with our mouths hanging open, too frightened to tell the truth and not able to think of a lie.

"We went to use the bathroom and saw a mouse," Cora piped up.

"My goodness, girls. You scared us to death. Everybody better get back to work and we'll set some traps. I haven't seen any signs of mice, but it is fall and they'll be coming inside," Mrs. Webb said.

As the teacher and the kids turned to go upstairs, Sandy, Cora and I exchanged silly grins.

"Mouse, I bet," Billy whispered in my ear, "More like hide-and-seek, if you ask me."

I gave him a "Keep your mouth shut, or I'll tell how the chair got broken" look. He made a motion with his hand by his lips like he was turning a key in a lock, which meant his lips were sealed. I could always count on Billy to know when to shut up.

* * *

Cora, Sandy and I always ate our lunch under the big oak tree in the back because the grass was nice and soft and the tree gave lots of shade and privacy. We'd always talk and laugh and have a good time. If Sandy was absent or had to stay in school the first fifteen minutes of recess to correct her work, Cora and I would trade sandwiches, fruit or cookies. Neither of us wanted to trade with Sandy and it would have been rude not to include her. Sandy only brought one sandwich a day, never any fruit and seldom a cookie. Her sandwich was made up of two slices of homemade bread and spread in the middle was either lard or mustard. Sandy didn't have any milk to wash those dry sandwiches down. We offered our milk to her once, but her feelings were hurt and she didn't eat with us for over a week.

We had just started unwrapping the wax paper from our sandwiches, Sandy's was wrapped in writing paper, when up came Karla and her friends.

"If it isn't the Three Musketeers," Karla smirked, as she sidled up to us.

"No, I think they're the Three Blind Mice," Marian, the redhead, twittered.

"You're both wrong," Donna, with the owl eyes, snickered. "They're the Three Little Pigs," and she started making grunting noises.

"You're absolutely right," Karla snapped. "Who else, but a pig, would eat lard sandwiches?" Karla started grunting like a pig, too. Pretty soon, all three of them were snorting like a whole pen of pigs.

"Shut up!" Cora shouted. She stood up to make herself look bigger, but it didn't help much. "Get out of here!"

"Tell you what, Miss Big Mouth, we'll leave you alone if you…" Karla thought for a few seconds. "…trade your sandwich with Sandy and eat the whole thing while we watch."

"No problem." Cora and Sandy exchanged sandwiches. Sandy had brought a mustard sandwich this time. "I love mustard sandwiches," Cora boasted.

I'll say one thing for Cora. She does some pretty stupid stuff, but she does it with style. I don't know what Karla was expecting Cora to do, gag or throw up. Cora took bite after bite of that dry sandwich and to rub the insult in even further, she made these little sounds of pleasure like this was the best sandwich she had ever eaten.

Meanwhile, Sandy was eating Cora's summer sausage sandwich on store-bought bread with crunchy pickles so fast, I don't think she even chewed.

When the last bite was swallowed, Cora opened her mouth so wide, to prove she had eaten it, you could probably see her tonsils.

Thoroughly disgusted, the three girls walked away. I whispered in Cora's ear when Sandy wasn't looking. "Was it pretty bad?"

"Yup," Cora replied as she bit into a big juicy apple.

* * *

It was a beautiful fall day in Wisconsin. The sky was bright blue and the sun was playing hide-and-seek behind the wispy clouds. Cora, Sandy, Judy and I had managed to get the swings this recess. They had shiny red painted boards and silver chains that were attached to an overhead pole. Sandy and I were sitting down in our swings and pumping with our legs. We were pretty high, but not as high as Cora and Judy, who were standing up and pumping their swings. I felt like a bird looking down from the sky at the world.

Tom, Ray and Fred were sitting on the teeter totters looking up at us, singing,

I see London, I see France
I see Cora's underpants. (Sometimes they put in Judy's name)
They aren't blue, they aren't pink
But, oh boy, do they stink!

That was ridiculous, because we girls had pulled slacks on under our dresses before we started swinging.

"Shut up!" Cora kept yelling back to them. I think if she had ignored them they would have gone away, but Cora likes a lot of attention.

I don't know if it was because Cora was paying attention to the boys and not what she was doing, or she slipped off the board, but the swing jerked and Cora went flying backward. She looked sort of graceful like a trapeze artist in the circus, except she didn't land gracefully on her feet like a trapeze artist. Cora landed on her side in a pile of leaves behind the swings and lay in a heap like a big rag doll. She didn't sound like she was in a circus, either, because she was screaming, "Mama! Mama!" at the top of her lungs.

"Is she dead?" Sandy asked, as we tried to stop our swings and go help her.

"Does she sound dead?" I asked irritably, too worried to put up with stupid questions.

By the time we got to Cora, she was surrounded by half the school, all talking at once trying to calm her down but only making her more frightened.

Cora looked terrible. The left side of her face was all scratched up and a big goose egg was forming on her forehead. Blood was running down her face into her left eye, which was beginning to swell shut. Her beautiful, blonde, curly hair was becoming sticky with blood and leaves were clinging to it. Her left arm was bent funny. Her beautiful yellow dress had the lace ripped on one side and was dirty and had blood spots on it. Her slacks were ripped in the knees.

Mrs. Webb came hustling up, assessed the situation and started giving orders. Dorothy was sent to the teacher's room for the emergency bag. Carol had to fill a clean pail with warm water. Arlene was to call Cora's parents from the phone list hanging on the wall by the phone. Susan was sent to bring back a blanket and all the clean rags she could find. Frank and Tom were sent into the woods to find a couple straight branches and strip off all the leaves and twigs to be used as a splint.

The rest of us stood around, not knowing what to do. Sandy and I hung on to each other's hands, afraid to let go. Mrs. Webb talked softly to Cora gently brushing her curls off her face. Cora stopped screaming and lay there shaking and moaning, tears running down her face.

Arlene got back first and announced that Cora's parents were on the way and that she had also called Holy Cross Hospital in Merrill so they'd have a doctor ready for Cora.

As soon as the supplies arrived, Mrs. Webb did a great job of cleaning up Cora and taking care of her injuries. Mrs. Webb asked Leroy to carry Cora into the school. Leroy is over six feet tall and very strong. His nickname is the Gentle Giant. With the help of the other eighth graders to support her arm and back, Leroy lifted her carefully, blanket and all.

Cora's mom and dad must have been flying in their truck, because they were driving into the school grounds just as we got Cora to the school door. They must have dropped whatever they were doing, because her dad was in his barn clothes and her mother had a dirty apron over her house dress. Cora's mother looked like she was going to faint she was so white. They talked quietly to Mrs. Webb and then her Dad carried her to the truck and she laid on the front seat with her head in her mother's lap.

Cora came to school the next day with a black eye, a big chunk of hair missing where a bandage was taped to her scalp and a white cast on her broken arm. We all took turns signing her cast. Susan printed, "Best Friends Always" on a piece of paper so I could copy it on Cora's cast and sign, "Jean."

Chapter Four
A New Student

One beautiful October day, a thin, lanky boy as colorful as the leaves on the trees appeared on the school steps. He had sandy red colored hair, a sprinkling of freckles on his nose and hands, sleepy-looking blue eyes and the only southern drawl we had ever heard at our school. He was wearing a red plaid, long sleeved cowboy shirt, tight blue jeans and cowboy boots. All the other boys had on dress pants and shirts. His hair was longer than the boys at our school and kept falling over his eyes. He was carrying a brown paper bag, which we later found out was his dinner.

The boy shook Mrs. Webb's hand like a grown-up, explaining that his name was Ned Gedding and that his family had just moved from Rock Ridge, Tennessee, into the area and were living across the highway at the end of the logging road in an old cabin there.

"If it please you kindly, ma'am, I'd like to start goin' to school here."

I didn't know if it pleased Mrs. Webb kindly, but it sure did please every other older female in that school. One look and every girl was instantly in love. You'd think he was Elvis Presley or something!

"Of course, Ned, what grade are you in?"

"I be goin' into seventh, ma'am. I ain't had a whole lot of book larnin', so's I probably ain't as good as y'all." At the mention of seventh grade, all the seventh grade girls smirked and looked pleased, especially Karla and her friends.

"I'm sure you'll do just fine, Ned. Besides, if you are behind in your studies, I'm sure someone will be willing to help you."

"I'll help him, Mrs. Webb," Karla burst out before she realized she had spoken out loud. The whole school laughed. The older girls rolled their eyes, the boys hooted and Karla turned as red as Ned's hair.

"I'm sure you'll be a big help," Mrs. Webb said, smiling. "In the meantime, Leroy, get a desk in the basement, a tall one. Junior, why don't you go, too?"

Ned was seated at the end of the seventh grade row, right across from my prissy sister. Susan pretended he wasn't even there, but every so often, she would sneak a look in his direction. Mrs. Webb gave him his textbooks and continued with her reading class. Susan, who was the best student in the school, was lost in the pages of her library book when she felt a tap on her arm.

"Would you have a pencil you could be lendin' me? I'll pay you back." Ned gave her that lopsided grin. Susan actually smiled back and brought out one of her one hundred ninety-nine pencils. Her motto was "Be prepared" probably long before the Boy Scouts ever thought about it. In fact, they probably stole the motto from my sister. From that moment on, he was constantly pestering my sister and she seemed to like it.

One day, Ned stopped Susan on her way into the school. He reached into his pocket and pulled out two bright blue pencils.

"Ma finally went to town and got me my school supplies," he said grinning.

"Thanks, Ned," Susan said softly, "but you only owe me one."

"Good deeds always multiply," he smiled.

"You mean if Susan kissed you, you'd have to give two back," Arlene interrupted, brushing past Susan as she went into school.

"Arlene!" Susan squealed, punching her friend in the arm.

Ned winked at Arlene and she winked back.

Ned was right. He wasn't very good in reading. He read very slowly and mispronounced most of the big words, but he made up for it when it came to arithmetic. Nobody, even Susan, could match him. He could add, subtract, multiply and divide two digits in his head. He was always the winner when the upper grades played "Around the World." Mrs. Webb always gave the winner a lollipop. Soon, these lollipops started appearing mysteriously in Susan's desk.

It didn't take long for the guys to accept Ned into their group once they discovered he had a cousin, who was a catcher in the American league. Billy even had a baseball card with his cousin's picture on it, until it disappeared. I saw it in Susan's underwear drawer and gave it back to Billy. Susan wouldn't speak to me for three days.

It was Ned's dream also, to be a professional baseball player, so every recess, the boys picked sides and played softball. Ned could catch better, hit farther and throw harder than anyone else in school. Besides being good at softball, he was kind.

One day, Jimmy, who was clumsy and pretty chubby, was almost in tears when he struck out for the fifth time in a row. Ned took Jimmy to a far corner of the ball field and pitched to him until he could get a piece of it every time. The boys kept asking Ned to play with them, but he'd always answer, "Thank you kindly, but me and Jimmy are busy practicin'." Ned also helped Jimmy learn to catch a ball without closing his eyes. Jimmy never did throw the ball too far, but it sure looked better than before. After three days of this, they joined the rest of the boys again on the main field.

It was Jimmy's turn at bat, everyone moved into the infield, in the fat chance that Jimmy might actually connect with the ball. Jake pitched the ball. Jimmy swung and whack! The bat hit the ball over the players' heads in a fly ball clean out to the fence. Jimmy made it to second. If he had been a little thinner, he could have made it home or third for sure. Everyone cheered and clapped him on the back as he ran the bases. I have never seen Jimmy smile so big in his life!

I don't know if Jimmy ever thanked Ned, but from that day, Jimmy followed Ned around like a puppy dog and wasn't picked last for softball games anymore.

Not long after Ned arrived, all the older girls suddenly got this desire to watch softball. They sat on the grassy bank above the ball diamond. Karla and her friends even tried cheerleading, throwing up dry leaves because they had no pom-poms. When they started cheering whenever Jake threw a wild ball, he'd finally had enough and told them to shut up because they looked like fools.

After a few days of sitting on the cold ground and being totally ignored, the girls started insisting that they had a right to play softball. It was a democracy and besides it was the school ball and bat, not just the boys'. The boys had no choice if they didn't want Mrs. Webb taking away the bat and ball, so the girls started playing, too. Susan and her friends and a few others weren't so bad. Dorothy, Susan's friend, could catch and pitch every bit as good as Jake, so she became a pitcher. Carol and Arlene took turns playing second base. Marian was good in the infield and the biggest surprise was that Susan turned out to be a power hitter. I think it was a bigger surprise to her than to the school.

Ned started calling her "Mickey" after Mickey Mantle. It caught on and pretty soon the whole school was calling her that. She acted like she was offended, but you could tell she was secretly pleased. Prior to that her nicknames had been "The Brain" or "Einstein." What girl wants to have the nickname of a strange looking guy with wild hair, no matter how smart he is? Thanks to Ned, she was even kind of popular.

Everyone seemed to really like Ned, except Frank and his brother Jake. Frank had been the leader before Ned had showed up. He had a big mouth and was really good at sports. He was cute and every month he had a new girlfriend. So when Ned showed up on the scene and all the girls had crushes on him, Frank took it personally. He hated Ned.

Frank was a hothead. One day, Dorothy struck out Frank three times in a row. Everyone was hooting and hollering and teasing him about being struck out by a girl.

Ned and Susan were laughing together near the backstop, when Frank suddenly threw the bat, just missing his brother Jake and stormed over to Ned and Susan.

"Leave my girl alone, hillbilly," Frank yelled, grabbing Ned by the shoulder and spinning him around.

Ned looked over at Susan questioningly.

"I'm not your girl, Frank, never have been and never will be!" Susan yelled in the disgusted tone she usually used only on Billy or me.

"Leave the pretty girl alone, Frank," Ned warned in his soft drawl.

"Oh, yeah, who's going to stop me? You, hillbilly?"

The whole school had gathered around. There is nothing like a good fist fight to get everyone's attention. I think secretly everyone who had ever been pushed around by Frank wanted him to lose, which was pretty much everyone except Jake, Karla and her friends. Somehow Karla's group had thought Susan had taken Ned away from Karla. How could Susan steal Ned from Karla, when Karla never had Ned in the first place, I wondered.

It wasn't much of a match to my way of thinking. Ned looked pretty weak, thin, tall and all arms and legs. Frank was shorter, stockier and strong as an ox. He helped his dad with chores on the farm morning and night and could throw a hay bale thirty feet. This wasn't going to be pretty, but I couldn't help but watch.

Frank took the first swing, hitting Ned in the chest and knocking him off his feet. Then Frank jumped on Ned's stomach and started pummeling jabs right and left to Ned's face and chest, most of them missing by a mile. After the first shock, Ned started punching back, most of his punches were connecting. It was pretty obvious that this wasn't the first fight Ned had ever been in. Ned tried turning Frank over, but Frank's extra weight kept Ned pinned to the ground. Finally, Ned managed to turn Frank, and there was a tangle of flying arms and legs rolling down the hill. Ned ended up on top and gave a mighty punch right in Frank's guts. Frank gave a huge groan as the wind was knocked out of him, and he just lay there. His nose was bleeding, and his clothes were ripped and covered with dried grass and leaves. Ned, on the other hand, only had a red bruise on his chin, which he was now rubbing gingerly and dried grass and leaves were clinging to his hair and clothing.

Ned reached down a hand to Frank still lying on the ground. After a moment, Frank accepted it and let Ned pull him to his feet.

"Where did you learn to fight like that?" Frank asked admiringly, wiping his bloody nose on his sleeve.

"Oh, we don't call that fightin' where I come from." Ned grinned. "We just call it southern justice."

"You're gonna get it now!" Jake warned. "She'll suspend you both for sure."

Someone must have tattled, because Mrs. Webb was headed down the hill followed by all the kids she had been doing corrections with in the schoolhouse. She looked like a mother hen followed by her chicks.

"Boys, stop that fighting right now!" Mrs. Webb scolded, marching with determination down the hill.

"We're not fightin', Mrs. Webb," Ned claimed, "We're just funnin'. Right, Frank?" Ned's hand was firmly placed in the small of Frank's back as a reminder that Ned could and would whip him again if he had to.

"Yeah, we're just funnin'," Frank mumbled, studying the toe of his boot.

"Are you sure?" Mrs. Webb glanced around the group.

"Yeah, just funnin'," a few mumbled while the rest just nodded. By the look on Mrs. Webb's face, you knew she didn't believe a word.

She sighed, glancing at Frank again, but it was clear Frank was sticking to his story. "I guess if no one is seriously hurt, we'd better get back to class. Recess is over."

Chapter Five
Halloween

"Hi, Jimmy!" I yelled as I passed him trudging up the hill. We both had our arms full with our Halloween costumes in a paper bag and dinner pails. Jimmy had a pillow stuffed under one arm. I wondered what costume Jimmy needed a pillow for? He was chubby already.

"Hi, Jeannie," Jimmy stopped and grinned at me as he rearranged his load.

Jimmy is round. Everything about Jimmy is round. He has a round body, a round head, and round chubby cheeks, the kind you want to grab and say "Grandma loves you". Jimmy loves to eat, probably more than anything else in the world. His whole family likes to eat, so they encouraged him in this pursuit. He gulps down his dinner and then tries to get everyone's leftovers. He's really a great guy and good natured. He laughs the hardest when Frank and Karla say mean things about him that sound funny. Instead of laughing, I'd like to see Jimmy get really mad and hit Frank right in that "pretty" face of his, but it'll never happen because Jimmy is too nice.

The Halloween party was today and the whole school had been in an uproar with preparation all week. There would be a party with games and food, a haunted house, even prizes for the best boy and girl costume and all the mothers were invited and of course, any younger brothers and sisters. We had been hard at work. The regular classes were forgotten as we cleaned and decorated the school for our guests.

The first, second and third graders were responsible for the decorations. The windows were all painted with tempera paint ghosts, witches, pumpkins and shaky looking haunted houses with bats flying out of the windows. At least, I think that's what they were supposed to be, sometimes it was hard to tell. I, alone, had cut out seven orange construction paper Jack-o-lanterns, four owls, seventeen bats, three black cats and two witches on broomsticks (These were hard to cut, and I cut off one tail and a broomstick, but we taped it back together). The other kids had been just as busy. Orange and black crepe paper streamers crisscrossed the entire classroom with our decorations hanging from them. There wasn't an empty place on a wall that didn't have a Halloween decoration.

The fourth, fifth and sixth graders were equally as busy. They were responsible for refreshments. There were large coffee cans filled with cookies with orange, white and yellow frosting safely stored between sheets of wax paper. Dozens of popcorn balls were made with sticky syrup and little bits of gum drops to make them look pretty. Yesterday, the fourth, fifth, and sixth graders were busy making chocolate and white cupcakes with orange and black sprinkles. Today they would make ground baloney sandwiches, caramel apples and witch's brew (fruit punch) because we didn't have a refrigerator.

At first, the boys didn't want to help with the baking.

"That's girl's work," Fred announced.

"Not really, Fred," Mrs. Webb said. "Some of the best French chefs are men."

"Frenchmen are sissies," Darlene, Marian's younger sister, said. She was always trying to act big and appear smarter than anyone else.

"Darlene, have you ever met a Frenchmen?" Mrs. Webb asked.

"No," Darlene mumbled, studying the floor around her shoes.

"Then I think you shouldn't be saying things you have no idea about. Words are very powerful and can cause a lot of damage. You need to think, Darlene, before you say things that could hurt others, even people you don't know."

Mrs. Webb touched Darlene's shoulder before she went to help someone else. Darlene stiffened up and looked pretty close to tears, but she'd never admit she was wrong. Instead, she stuck out her bottom lip and stomped over to her seat. She sat and pouted until she realized nobody cared if she was helping or not and she was missing out on all the fun.

While all these preparations were going on upstairs, the seventh and eighth graders were setting up a haunted house in the basement. The boys had strung four long wires in the center of the basement. Dark colored blankets hung from these wires. Any student not in seventh or eighth grade was supposed to stay away from this area. The upper graders had posted "DO NOT DISTURB" signs all over that area, but I bet every kid in school has made the excuse to use the bathroom when no one else was downstairs and crawled under the blankets and looked. I know I did. All that was there was a bunch of tables, chairs and desks stacked so there was a winding maze from one end to the other end of the curtained area. It didn't look scary to me. Every day, they brought bags of things to be used in the haunted house. Today we heard them practicing. Screams, moans and howls kept floating up the stairs and when you needed to use the bathroom, someone met you at the bottom of the steps, blindfolded you and led you to and from the bathroom.

After dinner and noon recess, we all changed into costumes, except the seventh and eighth graders. Even Mrs. Webb dressed up as Mrs. Santa Claus. See, I told you they looked a lot alike.

My costume was a combination of a pumpkin and a witch. My mother and Susan had sewn a skirt out of orange crepe paper. Then I pasted on black witches, black cats and bats. I had a black shawl and a black witch's hat made out of cardboard.

Cora had on her tap dance costume. It had a sparkly top and filmy full red skirt that flared out when she twirled. She twirled so much, she got dizzy and slammed into the wall. Cora wore her church shoes. Her mother wouldn't let her wear her tap shoes because of the wooden floors.

Roger was a cowboy with a holster, two cap pistols and a black cowboy hat. Teacher took away the caps because the mothers jumped every time they heard it, and the babies cried. That didn't stop Roger. He kept going around saying, "Stick 'em up! I'm a two-pistol, gun-totin' son-of-a-gun!" That kid watches way too many western movies.

John was wrapped in strips of a sheet to look like an Egyptian mummy. Instead of wrapping the strips around each leg separately, his brother, Tom, had wrapped both legs together. Poor John couldn't walk. He had to hop to get any place and he couldn't talk because his mouth was covered. That's the quietest I've ever seen John.

Darlene was wearing a cousin's old prom dress, which was miles too big on top. She had a big safety pin in the back. The dress was green and satin and would have been pretty if anyone but Darlene was wearing it. She had on matching high heel shoes which didn't fit at all. Her legs were all wobbly and she kept turning her ankles. On her head was a tinfoil and glitter crown. I don't know if she was the queen or Miss America.

Andy saw Darlene and covered his eyes and started screaming. "Quick! Take off your mask! It's too scary!"

Darlene wasn't wearing a mask.

"Very funny," she grumbled as she stumbled away. "Tell me when to laugh."

Karla's owl-eyed friend, Donna, was dressed like a peacock. She had a blue shirt and pants and three peacock feathers taped to her backside. That's just dumb.

Marian was actually pretty as a hula dancer. Her coppery hair fell over a Hawaiian shirt. She had a lei of paper flowers and a grass skirt made of green crepe paper cut in strips.

Everyone had a costume. Even Sandy came in her mother's old bathrobe and scuffed up slippers. She was holding a scruffy teddy bear.

"What are you?" I asked.

"A sleepwalker!"

There was everything from ghosts to vampires.

The big afternoon was finally here. Everything was ready. The only problem was that one of the Johnson twins had dropped a gallon of pickles, and the whole school smelled like a pickle factory. The windows were wide open, but the smell was still pretty strong by the time the mothers arrived.

The festivities started with the costume judging. The guests did the judging. I won first place for the girls, and Jimmy won for the boys.

Jimmy had on his dad's overalls stuffed with a pillow, so he looked enormous. He also had on a red flannel shirt, a big straw hat and a fake gray beard that hung over his stomach. Ralph's mother laughed so hard, tears were running down her face. I didn't think he was that funny. He looked like my grandpa.

We both received a long tube of candy corn with a witch's head on the top. Jimmy tore into his right away. I saved mine to share with Cora and Sandy later.

Then the games began. Thomas unwound the strips of sheet from John so he could play games too.

Mrs. Webb had drawn a huge witch on the chalk board and everyone was given a hat with a piece of tape on the back to put on her head. The only problem was that we were blindfolded and spun around. You didn't know where to put the hat. Frank almost put it on Cora's grandma's chest, so after that, when you were spun around, they pointed you in the right direction. That poor witch had that hat everywhere but on her head.

Next we formed two teams and had to pass an orange that we held under our chin without using our hands. Our team lost because Jimmy had too many chins and didn't have room for an orange, so every time it got to him, it rolled to the floor and we had to start over. Finally, the orange split and the other team won. The orange never did get to me. That wasn't much fun. The other team got all-day Holloway suckers. No one yelled at Jimmy this time, because his mother was watching. I was glad no one yelled because I knew he felt bad and his mother would have felt bad too.

I hated it when kids pick on someone because they're different. Jimmy got picked on because he's too fat and Arlene because she's too skinny. Susan was too smart, and Gary was too dumb. Leroy was too tall, and I was too short.

I didn't know why kids had to pick on someone who's different. I hated being a "too." I just wished I was like everyone else.

Then we dropped clothespins into a milk bottle. We had to stand on a chair and drop them directly into the bottle's mouth. Everyone said that wasn't fair because the little kids were shorter and therefore closer to the bottle. That didn't help me any. I didn't get any in. Cora got eleven in and won a coloring book. She thought it was such a big deal to win because she had a cast on one arm. I pointed out that you didn't need two arms to drop a clothespin in a bottle. You only needed to have a talent for that, and some of us had other talents that were more useful. Cora said I was a poor sport.

After that, we were each given half a paper pumpkin and had to find who had the other half. Fred had the other half that matched mine. After everyone had found their partner, we went outside to bob for apples and went against the person who matched our pumpkin half. There was a big metal washtub filled with water and apples.

I didn't stand a chance. Everyone knew that Fred had one of the biggest mouths and the hardest heads in the school. He wasn't afraid of getting wet either. He stuck his big old head under the water, pushing my head away and had a juicy chunk taken out of the apple before I even found one. He splashed up so much water that my crepe paper skirt fell apart. I felt like crying, but my mother said that judging was over and I should take it off anyway.

Cora couldn't bob for apples because she might get her cast wet. As I shook the water out of my hair, I told her not to worry. It wasn't any fun anyway.

After the games, the seventh and eighth graders went downstairs to set up the haunted house. When they were ready, the visitors were led downstairs one by one. Everyone had a turn, except a couple of grandmas, who said they really didn't want to tackle the stairs. After the mothers came up, they giggled like a bunch of school girls, but they wouldn't tell us anything.

Anyone who wasn't downstairs waited on the guests. We passed plate after plate of sandwiches and other goodies. At the rate things were disappearing, I was afraid we might run out of food, but I needn't have worried. There were tons more in the kitchen.

When our guests were served we stood around waiting to be called downstairs. Everyone was complimenting each other's mother by saying how pretty they were, or how young they looked, or how lovely their hair was. Everyone thought my mother had a beautiful smile, which she does. No one had said anything about Sandy's mother.

I think Sandy was starting to feel pretty bad. She wasn't talking much anymore and her smile seemed kind of fake. I tried to think of something I could compliment her mother about. I didn't want to out and out lie. I'm not a good liar, and Sandy would know right away, only making things worse.

Sandy's mom was thin as a stick, even after eleven kids, which is pretty amazing, if you ask me. She had small, dark eyes with bushy eyebrows that met over one of the longest noses I had ever seen. Her hair was black with lots of gray streaks. When she smiled, she had no teeth. Sandy said she was going to get some when they had more money. This didn't seem to stop her, though, from gumming down those sandwiches and treats one after the other. She had three scrawny little kids crawling over, under and around her chair. When one got too far away, Sandy would scoop them up and bring them back while her mother kept talking to the women around her. I know it was mean, but all I could think of when I looked at her was a witch, so of course, I couldn't think of a single compliment.

Finally, good old Judy, who was always happy and smiling and could always think of something good to say about everyone, saved the day. "Your mother sure has a pretty dress, Sandy," Judy said. Sandy relaxed, and a wide smile spread across her face.

"Yes, yes," we all chorused, just thankful that Sandy's feelings weren't hurt.

I learned a good lesson that day. There is always something nice to be said about everyone, even if you need to search for it sometimes.

Finally, it was my turn to go through the haunted house. The boys had all come upstairs saying, "Cool and groovy." The girls didn't seem quite so thrilled. Everyone had agreed to be quiet about the haunted house, so it would be a surprise for those who hadn't gone downstairs yet. and surprisingly everyone kept the secret. I was nervous. What if I fainted or was so scared I wet my pants? As soon as I reached the bottom of the steps, I was blindfolded and led into the haunted house.

"Welcome to my laboratory," a spooky voice whispered. "Would you like some eyeballs?" My hands were guided into a bowl filled with something round, slimy and slippery.

"How about some intestines?" another voice coaxed. "They're so fresh they are still moving." I felt something long, round and cool crawl over and around my hands. I pulled my hands out so fast, I hit the kid guiding me through the maze.

"Would you like a bite of a warm fresh heart? Listen, it's still beating." It sounded more like ticking than beating to me. "If you do not want a bite, I'll take one," the spooky voice said. I heard a squishy sound then something wet splattered all over my face. I screamed and jumped back. I heard a laugh. Then it sounded like someone covered the laughing person's mouth.

I was guided from table to table as each spooky voice told me about one creepy thing after the other. Finally, my blindfold was jerked off and right before my eyes were four floating heads. I screamed so loud the heads jumped. It was actually four kids dressed in black with flashlights under their chins. I was really glad when that was over.

When the students had all had a chance to go through the haunted house, we ate dinner. Everyone, especially the boys, kept saying things like, "This is the best brain sandwich I've ever eaten." It didn't stop anyone from wolfing down the good things the fourth, fifth and sixth grade had made.

Everyone said it was the best Halloween party ever!

Chapter Six
The New Teacher

November brought with it cold northern winds and bad news. Mrs. Webb announced that this would be her last week as our teacher. She was going to have a baby, and the doctor told her that her blood pressure was too high. She could lose the baby if she didn't get more rest. Everybody felt really rotten about her leaving, although nobody wanted her to lose her baby, of course. Some of the older girls even started crying. I didn't because I only knew her a few months. I figured it was too bad she has to leave. She was so nice, but nothing would really change. Weren't all teachers the same?

We spent that week secretly making "We'll Miss You" cards out of construction paper with pictures of teary eyed students waving good-bye.

On Friday afternoon of her last week, there was a knock on the door, and Marian's and Darlene's mother stood there holding a large white gift with blue and pink ribbons. Behind her were all the other parents, even my mom, holding similarly wrapped presents. The mothers had planned a baby shower with presents, food and even bottles of cold pop.

One by one, Mrs. Webb unwrapped all the soft, pretty little nightgowns, blankets, bonnets and tons of cloth diapers. I don't think the boys enjoyed it as much as the girls; because as the gifts were being passed around, Ray started playing the cha-cha with two baby rattles and Andy put a yellow booty on each ear and did some kind of Mexican hat dance without the hat.

Fred's mother had baked a big cake with white frosting and yellow icing trim. On the top of the cake was a long-legged, white plastic bird holding a diaper in his yellow bill with a little plastic baby in it.

"That's the stork," Cora stated to Sandy and me. "They bring babies."

"I don't think so," Sandy said. "My momma had eleven babies, and I never once saw any big old bird flying around. Her belly jest keeps gettin' bigger."

"If storks bring babies," I interrupted, "why does Mrs. Webb have to stop teaching?"

For once, Cora didn't have an answer.

* * *

"I am your new teacher," the tall, thin woman standing behind the teacher's desk at the front of the room announced. "My name is Mrs. Craig."

Mrs. Webb had been soft and round, whereas Mrs. Craig was all angles. Mrs. Craig had a long horse shaped face with high pointed cheek bones and a pointy chin.

Her small, beady brown eyes peered through thick dark framed glasses which were perched at the end of her stick-like nose. She had thin lips which disappeared when she smiled, which we found out wasn't very often. Her short, permed hair had streaks of gray running through it. She looked old enough to be my grandma, but it turned out that she and my mother were the same grade in high school. I guess teaching really ages a person.

"I know you will miss Mrs. Webb, but I'm your teacher now and things will be done my way." Mrs. Craig then hung up a wooden paddle behind her desk. On the paddle written in big letters was "BOARD OF EDUCATION." There also were two little cartoon characters. One was a fat man dressed in a suit paddling a little boy with the Board of Education. The little boy was yelling and the man looked happy. Nobody laughed.

Everything went smoothly until it was time for my class to read.

"Today, children," Mrs. Craig stated, "we're going to learn about poems. Some poems rhyme and some don't."

Roger started wildly waving his hand. "Teacher, teacher, I know a poem my brother taught me."

"My name is not teacher, it's Mrs. Craig. Teacher is my profession, not my name."

Roger looked confused. "Teacher, I know a poem."

Mrs. Craig sighed. "Would you like to say it Roger?"

"Yup," and he stood up and recited,

"I'm not a chicken plucker

But I'm a chicken plucker's son,
And I'll pluck chickens
Until the chicken plucker's come."

Upon hearing Roger's poem, the entire school started laughing, except for Mrs. Craig, who was scowling. Encouraged, Roger repeated it.

"I'm not a chicken plucker
But I'm a chicken plucker's son,
And I'll pluck chickens
Until the chicken plucker's come."

Some of the boys began hooting, and Andy even started rolling around on the floor.

"Stop that right now!" Mrs. Craig screamed. "I forbid you to carry on like that!" Everyone turned to look at the teacher. Mrs. Craig was standing. The tips of her fingers were jammed into the top of the table. Her face was red, and she was bug-eyed. "Roger, come over here." She grabbed a small wooden stool and set it in the corner. "Now you sit here and think about what you did wrong."

The problem was that Roger, or anyone else in the school, didn't know what Roger did wrong. Mrs. Webb always laughed along with the class when someone did something silly, and then we'd get back to work, but Mrs. Craig made such a big deal over something so small, we didn't know what to think.

Maybe Mrs. Craig had forgotten about Roger or maybe she wanted to make an example of him, but he was in that corner for about an hour. The first fifteen minutes went fine. Then Roger started getting restless. He laid on his stomach on the stool. He laid on his back on the stool. Then he stood on the stool and pretended to be directing a band. Next he crawled under the stool and pretended the stool was his shell and he was a turtle, sticking his head and hands and feet in and out of the shell.

While all this was happening, Mrs. Craig had her back to Roger and was busy teaching class. Everyone else, though, kept one eye on Roger so as not to miss anything. No one laughed for fear of being punished by Mrs. Craig. When she finally remembered Roger, he had removed his shoes and was lying on his back on the stool walking his stocking feet up the wall as high as he could go and then back down.

"Roger, stop that! You bad, bad boy!" she yelled.

Then my sister Susan stood up and looked the new teacher in the eye. I didn't know what had come over Susan. Maybe having Ned as a boyfriend made her brave, or maybe she couldn't stand seeing a little kid being picked on.

"He's not a bad boy," Susan stated calmly. "He just gets jumpy." She smiled at Mrs. Craig. "Mrs. Webb used to say Roger's brain thinks so fast that sometimes his body tries to keep up with his brain and that makes him wiggly. It's not a bad thing. It's just how he is."

Mrs. Craig's face was beginning to turn red again. Fire flashed in her eyes and her chin pushed out toward Susan. She came over and towered over my sister.

"Listen, young lady. I don't need any sass from you. I'm the teacher here, not Mrs. Webb, not you, just me. Roger, go back to your seat. Susan can take your place for talking back to a teacher."

Roger picked up his shoes and carried them in his arms back to his desk. He looked confused. He was used to being scolded, but what had Susan done?

Susan hesitated a moment, opened her mouth as if to speak, decided not to, clenched her jaw, looked straight at Mrs. Craig and walked into the corner with her head high and her shoulders back and sat on the stool facing the wall.

The entire school was shocked. No one had ever been punished by Mrs. Webb by being sent to the corner and certainly not quiet bookworm Susan. No one said anything for fear of being sent to another corner, or worse yet, getting the "BOARD OF EDUCATION" applied to the seat of their pants. Ned tried getting Susan's attention when Mrs. Craig wasn't watching, but Susan refused to look at him and just stared straight ahead. Frank, Karla and her friends kept smirking at each other as if this was a big joke.

Susan sat in the corner, her back as straight and stiff as the yardstick. Mrs. Craig continued with her lessons. Everyone kept stealing glances at Susan in the corner. After a few minutes, her shoulders began to shake, and dark spots appeared on the sleeves and skirt of her dress. She sniffed quietly to herself and sometimes used her sleeve to wipe her eyes.

Billy went to the bubbler, and as he passed Susan, he dropped his clean handkerchief in her lap and lightly tapped her shoulder. Without turning around, Susan reached up and gave his hand a little squeeze.

At recess, none of the older kids were playing the usual games. They were standing in two groups, one group was around Susan and the other around Karla. Both groups were discussing the new teacher and what had just happened.

I went with my friends to jump rope. Sandy and Cora were turning the rope. I was on the part of the Teddy Bear rhyme where "Out goes you!" and I had to run out without tripping, when I saw Karla, Donna and Marian saunter over to Susan's group. I knew this wasn't good.

Susan was just saying, "I've never been so embarrassed or humiliated in my life."

"What a witch," Carol chimed in.

"Well, if it isn't Miss Big Mouth!" Karla screeched. "You better watch what you say about the new teacher, Susan. She's got your number."

"How's it feel not to be teacher's pet, Susan?" Donna giggled.

"How's it feel to be dumb and ugly?" Susan retorted.

Donna stood there with her big lips hanging open, not being able to think of anything smart to say back to Susan.

Karla stepped into the circle of Susan's friends and positioned herself directly in front of Susan, separating her from her friends.

"Bet you don't think you're so smart now, Susan, do you?" Karla stated with a toss of her ponytail. "I'm glad we finally have a decent teacher, one who's not afraid to stand up to you, even if your dad's on the school board. I bet you won't get all those A's now. You'll actually have to earn your good grades. You think you're so smart, always bossing everyone around and showing off."

I expected Susan to turn away and ignore Karla like she usually did. I think that's what Karla expected too, but Susan had been pushed as far as anyone was going to push her today.

"I bet you do like the new teacher, Karla. You're a lot alike. You're both mean and pick on little kids. No wonder no likes you. You only have two pathetic friends." Susan nodded toward Marian and Donna as they huddled behind Karla. "One's your cousin," Susan glanced at Marian, "and probably has no choice, and the other," Susan glared at Donna, "is afraid of you."

"Shut up, Susan!" Karla yelled, and she grabbed Susan by her ponytail.

Susan twisted around and grabbed a hand full of Karla's hair.

Someone must have told the teacher, because at that moment, Mrs. Craig came tearing out of the school. She could sure move a lot faster than Mrs. Webb. She grabbed each girl by the arm and demanded that they let go of each other's hair, but not before they each gave one more hard jerk.

"There will be no fighting in my school. I'm calling your parents, and we will get to the bottom of this rule breaking today."

When Susan heard that, all color drained from her face. We had the type of parents that thought the teacher was always right, even when the teacher was wrong. On the other hand, Karla's parents felt their precious child never did anything wrong and the teacher was never right.

Right after the buses left, both sets of parents came to school. Billy and I stayed also. We were sent outside to wait. The meeting lasted over an hour. When the meeting was over the adults were smiling and shook hands. The girls were crying.

What happened was that both girls had to apologize to each other for the mean things they had said to each other. Then Susan had to apologize to old stony-faced Mrs. Craig. Mrs. Craig also apologized to Susan for overreacting. When it was time for the parents to talk, they expressed how disappointed they were that their young ladies had acted so poorly. The girls would be punished by missing all recesses and noon hours for a month and read and write book reports on each book they read. This was great for Susan, whose hobby was reading. This was not great for Karla, whose hobby was gossiping.

Chapter Seven
Christmas Program Practice

I watched Gary run to catch up with the rest of the kids who were going to play Auntie-I-Over by the front porch that now looked like a shed. It was typically cold and overcast for this time of year. The sky was an omen of the snows to come. A bitterly cold wind attacked from the north. Gary buttoned the only two buttons remaining on his thin, brown jacket. He tucked a long, green, knotty-looking scarf around the opening at his throat where there should have been a button. He jammed a matching hat over his greasy black hair. Gary had no mittens. His mittens from last year now fit one of his younger brothers or sisters so they had been handed down. Hopefully his grandma would have another pair knitted by the time the snow started flying. It was easier to hold on to the ball if a person wasn't wearing gloves or mittens. Anyway, that's what Gary told everyone, but his hands were the worse for wear because of it. They were rough, red and chapped.

Dirt was embedded in the cracks. His hands probably hurt, but he never complained.

Gary loved playing Auntie-I-Over. He was always the first chosen because he could catch, run and throw better than anyone. Gary wasn't good at schoolwork, but he was good at this.

It wasn't a good day for this game. The wind kept blowing the ball off course. Plus, the wind was howling so loud it was impossible to hear anyone yell and know when the ball was coming.

Gary missed three thrown balls, and no one else was any better. Finally, Gary caught the ball and sprinted around the porch with his teammates in close pursuit. He spotted David and nailed him right in the back. He recaptured the ball before anyone else could and hit Carol in the arm. Once more, he picked up the ball and hit Junior in the shoulder.

"Hey, man!" Andy yelled. "Not so hard, that ball feels like a bullet today."

Gary saw David rubbing his back where the ball had hit, and Carol had pushed up her coat sleeve and was inspecting a round red mark on her arm.

"Sorry!" Gary shouted over the wind. "I guess I don't know my own strength."

"You don't have any strength," Andy teased, slugging Gary playfully in the arm. "The ball's frozen."

"Let's play merry-go-round tag instead!" Carol shouted, running toward the merry-go-round. "Last one there is a rotten egg."

For once, everyone was glad when the bell rang ending recess.

Mrs. Craig had a large pile of papers stacked on top of her desk. She announced that it was time to start preparing for the Christmas program coming up in the middle of December. There would be plays, poems, group and individual songs, instrumental and vocal solos and as something different, we would square dance. Since we had a lot to prepare for and only a month to do it, we would practice some every day. She then passed out play parts and poems. Cora would say the welcoming poem for the program and I would say the closing poem. Sandy, John and Roger would have small parts in a play.

We started by practicing the Christmas songs. I and everyone else knew most of them by heart. I thought we were doing pretty good until it came to *Deck the Halls* and the boys couldn't or wouldn't get their fa la las right. Next we tried that song that says,

> *"Chestnuts roasting on an open fire.*
> *Jack Frost nipping at your nose."*

The boys kept saying,

> *"Coconuts roasting on an open fire.*
> *Jack Frost nibbling at your toes."*

It was funny the first time Andy did it. Then all the boys joined in. By the seventh time, the girls were annoyed and so was Mrs. Craig. The boys still thought it was the funniest thing they ever heard. Finally, Mrs. Craig had to threaten them with phone calls home before they knocked it off.

Each day we practiced something different in the afternoon. The most fun was practicing for the square dances. The teacher arranged us by height. I was stuck with John. Cora was with Roger. Teacher put Gary with his sister Sandy, even though he was quite a bit taller, because (although it was never said) nobody wanted to hold his hands. Susan was hoping to get Ned as a partner, but instead ended up with Ray, who is so shy that he turned red every time they had to hold hands. Much to Susan's dismay and Karla's pleasure, Karla was partnered with Ned.

My group was learning the *Virginia Reel* and the older group was doing a harder dance to the song *Red River Valley*. Cora and I thought it was unfair that the older grades always got to do the fun things. Judy said not to worry, that we would get our turn when we were older. She said it just seemed like more fun because we couldn't do it.

One afternoon when we were singing a rousing chorus of *We Wish You a Merry Christmas,* Roger shouted, "Look, it's snowing!"

We all looked out the window and, sure enough, soft, white flakes were gently drifting to the ground. Everyone wanted to get a closer look, but we were afraid to join Roger at the window for fear of being yelled at by Mrs. Craig.

Everyone anxiously looked at her, and she responded with one of her rare smiles.

"Go ahead and look," she said. "I guess the first snow of the season is a pretty big deal. It won't hurt to take a five-minute break."

As we watched, the snow started coming down heavier. The ground was already covered, and we couldn't wait until recess to go outside. Mrs. Craig said that if we practiced really hard without any fooling around for the next hour, we could have an extra-long recess. That was the best practice we ever had! We went through every song, play and poem without any major mistakes or the usual foolishness from the boys or pouting from the girls.

It took Cora and me a while to get our dresses tucked into our snow pants and our shoes tucked into our boots and zip them up. Our long scarves were wrapped around our necks and half our face and then tucked into our coats. We put on our warm winter hats and finally pulled on our thick homemade mittens. Everyone had beat us outdoors.

We headed for an area of clean fresh snow and immediately laid on our backs and brushed our arms up and down at our sides making angel wings and brushed our legs and feet sideways and together again to make the angel's skirt. We laid there for a while just enjoying the pretty flakes floating down and landing on our eyelashes, tongue and face.

"Go ahead, get up," Cora encouraged.

"No, you get up," I insisted.

This was the hard part, getting up without wrecking the snow angel. Whoever got up first could help pull the other person up and chances were if you were helped, you'd have a perfect angel. Neither of us wanted to go first.

"I know," I said. "Let's both go on the count of three." That's just what we did.

I dug my heels into the snow, pushed off with my butt and had a near perfect angel. Cora had pushed her fist down in one of the wings, so hers didn't look quite so good, but we were happy and exclaimed about what good angel makers we were. When we grew up, we would go all over the world making snow angels in Germany, France and even England. Teacher had been reading about the Christmas customs in those countries. We weren't sure if they had snow in all those places, but they must have. Who'd want to live any place that didn't have snow!

This wasn't a packing snow so we couldn't make snowmen or snowballs. So we joined the other kids on the fox and goose track they had made in the snow on the softball diamond. Cora and I had so many clothes on that we could barely move, so we were always getting tagged, but it was just fun running and screaming with the other kids.

The bell rang, and we all headed for the warmth of the school. Our faces were red and cold, but the rest of us was toasty warm from all the exercise. Just as I unwound my scarf and shook off the remaining snow, David ran by with a fresh handful of snow and rubbed it in my face.

"Face wash!" he yelled as he sprinted by me into the building.

What a brat, but he is cute with those brown eyes and black hair.

* * *

Sheila and her sisters each brought a huge plastic ring called a hula hoop to school. Their grandma from Milwaukee, had brought them when she visited at Thanksgiving. Sheila had a pink one, Peggy had a green one, and Cheryl had a blue one. The idea was to put this plastic ring around your waist and do the hula to keep it up. Cheryl and her sisters were pretty good, but the rest of us were lousy. Poor Jimmy got stuck in Peggy's hoop when he tried. Dorothy and Frank had to jiggle it off of him. He laughed, but I know he was embarrassed. I sure would have been. Every recess, we took turns with the hula hoops. I finally was able to keep it going for two minutes. That's a lot of hula hooping!

Teacher announced that there would be a contest to draw the picture for the front of the Christmas program. It could only be drawn with pencil because color wouldn't show up on the mimeograph machine. She would run them off on red or green paper to make them colorful.

Everyone went to work quietly drawing the prize winning picture, or so they hoped. Mrs. Craig put a Christmas record on the record player, a 75 RPM, and we listened to all the old favorite Christmas songs as we worked. Some kids sang along. When everyone was finished, we went up to the front of the room and showed our picture for all to see. Then we would vote on the nicest picture.

When it was my turn, I went to the front and held up the picture I had drawn of a Christmas tree. One side had five points, and the other had four. The tree was too tall for the paper so the tip of the tree tilted to one side with the star hanging on for dear life. Karla and her group snickered until Mrs. Craig gave them a crabby look. I didn't know what they were laughing at. This is how our tree at home looked pretty much each year if Daddy didn't cut off the top or bottom.

Nobody laughed when Gary bashfully came up and held his drawing in his red rough hands. We gasped. Gary had drawn the stable with a beautiful Virgin Mary holding baby Jesus on her lap, while a proud Joseph stood in the background.

We finished looking at everyone's picture, but we all knew who should win. Gary got every vote but three. Karla got three votes for her picture of a stocking stuffed with toys and candy canes.

Gary received a drawing tablet, a large pack of colored pencils and a box of one hundred forty-four crayons. I noticed Gary never took them home but always kept them safely in his desk. I guess if you have ten brothers and sisters, you need to have something just for you.

Chapter Eight
A Christmas Surprise

Preparations were in full swing for the Christmas program. Our practices took up most of the afternoon and no one was using a script any more for their part. The songs were all memorized, and only Gary couldn't remember what came next in the *Virginia Reel*, so Sandy had to drag him around to end up in the right place at the right time.

It was below zero, so Mrs. Craig let us stay in for recess. Cora and I were playing the card game Slap Jack at her desk. I usually won because Cora was always so busy talking she forgets to slap, just like today.

Mrs. Craig had placed all our names in a coffee can for gift exchange and went around the room letting us pull names. When she was sure we didn't have our own name, she went on to the next person. I was hoping to get Cora, but instead I got Gary's name. What do you get someone who needs everything? He could use mittens, a scarf, a warm hat, or drawing supplies.

Mrs. Craig said we weren't supposed to tell anyone whose name we had, but I'm sure she didn't mean that you couldn't tell your best friend. So I told Cora who I had and she told me that she had Diane. Diane is a tomboy, so Cora wanted to get her a softball glove.

"How can you get a softball glove for one dollar?" I asked. That was the money limit we were supposed to pay.

"How much do softball gloves cost?" she asked.

"I don't know," I replied, "but I'm sure they cost more than a dollar."

"Who do you think has your name?" she asked.

"I don't have any idea. Do you know who has yours?" Cora had this superior look on her face, like when she knows an answer in class and I don't, which isn't that often.

"Yes." Cora just grinned at me.

"Who? You've got to tell me. I'd tell you if I knew who had me."

Cora looked around to make sure that no one was near enough to overhear. "Keith."

"You're kidding? Are you sure?"

Cora had the biggest crush on Keith. He was in fourth grade with dark straight hair, brown eyes and bushy eyebrows and the longest eyelashes I've ever seen except on a baby doll one time. He was pretty quiet and much more into sports than girls, but Cora had convinced herself that he had a crush on her too.

"How do you know?" I pushed.

"I don't," she replied, "but after he drew his name, he looked in our direction."

"Maybe he was looking at me."

She didn't even bother to answer that.

* * *

Mrs. Craig had been working with the third grade reading group. They had been reading a story about a teddy bear with a crooked leg. Santa had put the bear back on the shelf because he didn't think any child would want it. The bear crawls off the shelf into Santa's sack of toys when Santa isn't looking. On Christmas Eve, they come to the house of a little girl who has a brace on her leg, and the little bear crawls into her arms while she is sleeping. She wakes up in the morning and is thrilled that the little bear is just like her and loves him forever.

"What's your teddy bear look like and what's his name?" Mrs. Craig asked Judy.

"His name is Teddy."

"Mine, too," Carlene interrupted.

"He's pink," Judy continued as if no one had spoken. "He has black glass eyes and nose and he had a blue ribbon, but I lost it last summer. I sleep with him every night. He stays on my pillow during the day."

Then Carlene told about her teddy bear that was brown and shaggy with a red ribbon that she still had and she looked at Judy.

Next she went on to the Johnson twins. She smiled at Matthew, the nicer of the two twins. You could tell the twins apart because Matt's face was a little rounder than Mark's. Mark was meaner too. He carried a black dinner pail that had a sticker on it that said, "Hair today and gone tomorrow." There was a picture of a guy with lots of hair then next to him was a guy who was bald.

"Matthew, what kind of teddy bear do you have?"

"We don't got no teddy bears," Matthew stated.

"You mean you don't have *any* teddy bears," Mrs. Craig said, for the moment more interested in his grammar than what he was saying.

"Nope," Mark interrupted. "We ain't got any teddy bears and never have. Jesse, Sara, or baby Mary ain't got any either."

Mrs. Craig looked surprised but kept bravely plowing forward. "Maybe Santa will bring you each a teddy bear," she said.

Both boys sadly shook their heads.

"Nope," Matthew whispered.

"We're not having Christmas this year," Mark stated.

I couldn't believe what I had just heard! Even Sandy and Gary's family had some kind of Christmas. Their mother went to work at the wreath factory in town for a couple months and every child in the family got one thing. They had a big meal of venison, one of the older brothers or father had shot during deer hunting season, vegetables from their garden and even pumpkin pie. Sandy had just told Cora and me all about it.

Not to have Christmas was unheard of — no tree, no presents, no meal. The whole school had stopped whatever they were doing and listened. No one could believe their ears!

"Mommy's too sick," Matthew whispered, "and Daddy said Grandma can't handle a new baby…"

"And Christmas, too," Mark piped in, finishing his brother's sentence, which they often did.

I saw their mother through the window last week waving good-bye to the boys when they got on the bus. She looked terrible. She was really thin, super pale, and her cheek bones poked out of her face. She had on a colorful scarf, because it looked like she didn't have any hair!

I talked to Momma that night, and she said Mrs. Johnson had a really bad sickness that was eating up her body. The problem was that she had had to wait to take any medicine until baby Mary had been born, and that was two months ago. Momma said the doctors were giving Mrs. Johnson medicine now, but it was too late and she wasn't going to make it. She said I should be very nice to Matthew and Mark, even when Mark was being naughty and shoved in line or hit me in the arm, because this was a hard time for the family. I started to cry, and Momma just held me, stroking my hair. I couldn't imagine being without my mother, and now the twins wouldn't have Christmas either.

Just then the phone rang. It was Mrs. Craig. She was calling up all the families in the school district, and together we would give that family a Christmas like they never have seen. No one was to say anything about it at school for fear that the twins would find out about the surprise.

My family went Christmas shopping for the whole Johnson family. It was so much fun. We bought a different truck for each of the boys, Matthew, Mark and Jesse. For Sarah, we found a baby doll with a tiny baby bottle and a little nightgown and rattle for baby Mary. We decided on slippers for the mother and grandmother and work gloves for the dad and grandpa. We carefully wrapped each present. I wanted so much to tell Cora, but Momma said that good works shouldn't be bragged about. It takes away what is special about giving.

At last, Saturday arrived, and the presents, along with a ham and Momma's special fruitcake, were all loaded in the car. I hoped the parents wouldn't be too proud to accept the help.

When we arrived at the house the driveway and road were packed with cars. Every family from Tug Lake School had decided that this brave little family was going to have a wonderful Christmas this year. I saw Sandy and Gary's mom and dad carrying in a nice looking tree that they had cut down in their woods and a big plate of decorated cookies. Mrs. Craig and her husband were unloading five teddy bears of different sizes and color from the trunk of their car with a variety of colorful wrapped packages. Everybody was waving to each other and shouting "Merry Christmas!" as they carried in armfuls of food and presents.

"Santa sure was busy last night," Mr. Johnson, a big man with a scruffy black beard, boomed as he shook everyone's hand, even the kids, as he welcomed them at the door of the screened porch. Their little black-and-white mutt was the official welcoming committee. He finally gave up barking in favor of jumping on everyone and licking whatever part he could reach.

The Johnsons had a tiny house that smelled like a combination of wet diapers, medicine and baby powder. The house was not built to welcome so many people. We were crammed together like the popcorn in a popcorn ball.

Mrs. Johnson was sitting in a corner of the couch against a pile of pillows holding Jesse on one side and Sarah on the other. She was so thin and was wearing a ratty pink bathrobe, which hung off her shoulders. She had absolutely no hair on her head. I tried not to look, but I had never seen anyone without hair before. Quickly, Arlene's mother put on Mrs. Johnson's head a soft white hat that she had knit. Tears of happiness cascaded down Mrs. Johnson's thin pale face as she kept saying, "This is wonderful. How can we ever thank you?"

Mrs. Craig was taking pictures with her Brownie camera that she later put in an album for the family. The twins, in matching blue cowboy pajamas, just stood watching the older students trim the tree and stack all the presents under it. Grandma sat in a rocker with a tiny baby in a nest of pink blankets.

After all the women had admired the baby and the men had discussed the weather, we all left. I felt better that day giving those presents to that family than I ever did getting any presents of my own. I think everyone else felt the same, judging from all the smiles.

Chapter Nine
The Christmas Program

We no longer had our regular classes. Everything revolved around preparing for the Christmas program. Mrs. Craig said that we were learning skills, but not those found in textbooks. We were learning the skills of teamwork and cooperation.

Frank and Jake's father and two older brothers set up a seven-foot, blue spruce Christmas tree in the front corner of the classroom. The big boys put the colored lights on the tree. Leroy stuck a white light in the star and placed it at the very top.

The whole school was busy making decorations. We glittered pine cones and hung them from the tree with shiny red and green ribbons. Next, we made angels out of paper cups, little Styrofoam balls for heads, cardboard wings, a pipe cleaner halo and a stapled ribbon on the back to hang them on the tree. Two white and three red pipe cleaners were twisted together to make candy canes.

Finally came the chains.

The younger kids sat at the back reading table making colorful chains out of brightly colored construction paper. Then all the little chains were put together and circled from the bottom of the tree to the top and back down again.

The older kids were at the front reading table using long skinny needles to string popcorn and cranberries onto long thin fishing line. I think more popcorn went on the floor and in their stomachs then on the chains. It's hard to put the popcorn on without breaking it, so they mostly ended up with cranberry chains.

It was a festive time. Mrs. Craig supplied us with Christmas cookies and popcorn to eat while we worked and she played Christmas songs in the background on the record player. Everyone was in a good mood (except teacher looked a little ornery), teasing good naturedly and telling stupid jokes:

*"Why did Santa cross the road?
To catch the chicken for his Christmas dinner."*

We put all the decorations on the tree and covered it with long silvery icicles. Mrs. Craig turned off the room lights. The tree lights twinkled red, orange, white, blue, and green in the corner. It was the prettiest Christmas tree I had ever seen. For a moment no one said a word just enjoyed the beautiful sight. Then everyone started talking all at once.

Finally, Mrs. Craig got us organized and we started program practice. We were supposed to go straight through the practice, just as we would tonight, while Mrs. Craig timed us.

The program started with Cora's opening poem. Cora stood in front of everyone, took a deep breath and cleared her throat. It sounded like she was coughing up a fur ball. The older girls rolled their eyes. I sure hope she didn't do that tonight.

Next came the opening songs sung by the entire school. Everyone lined up in the library and walked in by rows. The tall kids in the back, middle sized in the middle and of course, the shortest kids, which included my class in the front. The songs were sung loudly and with spirit as Mrs. Craig pounded out the tunes on the piano, which now replaced her desk.

The first play was about a little girl who only wanted a stray kitten for Christmas that she had seen on the streets. Christmas morning, she finds the little kitten curled up under the Christmas tree. I have no idea how Dorothy managed to talk Mrs. Craig into letting her bring her new little kitten, but she did. Tinker Bell had been quiet all morning, a gray little ball of fluff curled into a corner of the cardboard box in which Dorothy had brought her. As soon as Dorothy took the surprise kitten out of the box, Tinker Bell started complaining. The louder the actors talked, the louder Tinker Bell complained. Finally, thoroughly disgusted with the whole thing, Tinker Bell took a bounding leap off Dorothy's lap and landed on the Christmas tree. Every time someone reached for her, she dove higher and deeper into the tree. Dorothy had to climb up the step ladder and pull her out. So much for Tinker Bell's acting career, she was replaced by a stuffed cat, and I don't think Tinker Bell even cared. She was put back in her box, and we never heard another meow from her. That whole drama had set us back fifteen minutes.

Next, Andy played "Silent Night" on the accordion. It's hard to play. It's not exactly my choice of instrument for that song. I'd rather hear a polka played on the accordion, but Andy said that he didn't know any Christmas polkas.

After Ned played *Skater's Waltz* on the harmonica (It wasn't even half bad), my group performed the square dance called the *Virginia Reel*. Everything went extremely smooth, even the part where you meet your partner and go under an arch formed by the other dancers' hands.

Then the taller kids took their places for their square dance. I don't know if it was the fact that Tinker Bell had loosened the tree in its stand; or if it was due to all the foot stomping in the square dance, but right during the first chorus that seven foot Christmas tree came crashing down right on top of Karla.

Ned saw the tree start to fall and yelled, "Watch out!" while trying to drag his partner, Karla, to safety. Poor Karla had her back to the tree and was completely taken by surprise. It had smashed her face first into the floor. All that could be seen of Karla was one arm and one leg. Everyone rushed over and the boys lifted the heavy tree off of Karla. A miracle took place that day in that one-room country school. The trunk of the tree had narrowly missed Karla by inches. She had been knocked to the floor by the weight of the branches. Ned had saved her life!

Karla was as mad as a wet cat. It didn't seem like anything was broken as she rushed to the long mirror in the hallway, swearing words I had never even heard before. Mrs. Craig didn't even tell her to be quiet. Mrs. Craig was so happy that Karla wasn't killed! Karla screamed when she saw herself in the mirror. Blood was pouring out of her nose and onto her blue sweater. A bump was forming on the bridge of her nose and another lump on her forehead. Scrapes and bruises were all over her arms and legs. The worst damage was that she had broken off one of her permanent front teeth.

While everyone was rushing around to help Karla by offering handkerchiefs and putting ice on her bumps, Mrs. Craig was able to reach Karla's dad. Her dad came in torn work overalls and a red and black jacket that looked like a long sleeved shirt with a black knit hat on his head. He looked over the situation, let out a whistle, slapped Karla on the back and exclaimed, "Holy, Bee-Jesus, girl, you look like you've been in a bar fight!"

For the first time that day, everyone saw humor in the situation and laughed so hard, we had to hold our sides and bellies; they ached with laughter. Karla gave everyone a dirty look and stomped out to the family truck.

By the time the boys had strung a wire around the tree and attached it to the wall and the girls had done their best to untangle the icicles and repair the squashed decorations, it was dinner time. Everyone grabbed their pails, ate a hurried dinner and headed outside to wear off some energy.

The snow-covered knoll the schoolhouse sat on, was just right for sliding today. A few kids had brought their wooden sleds, but most of us just used big slabs of cardboard under our backsides to slide down the hill. A couple kids rode down the hill on shovels. I could curl up on the shovel but the handle kept banging me in the head.

After dinner recess, Mrs. Craig continued where we left off. She chose Lois to take Karla's part in the square dance, in case Karla couldn't come tonight. Lois is a mousy kind of girl. She has straight brown hair, brown eyes and is afraid of everything. She's nice and a really smart girl. Lois doesn't talk much, because when she is nervous or tired, she stammers. Lois had no idea what to do in the square dance, but after three practices, it wasn't her making the mistakes.

Next Donna played *Away in the Manger,* on the piano, only having to start over twice. Sheila played *Santa Claus is Coming to Town* on the piano without any mistakes.

Matthew and Mark sang *Jingle Bells* while enthusiastically shaking sleigh bells. In fact, Mark was so enthusiastic he almost knocked himself out with them.

Frank and Jake played on their guitars and sang *How Much is the Doggie in the Window?* I told Cora that wasn't any Christmas song. She said that sure it was because children got puppies for Christmas all the time, and besides, this was the only song Frank and Jake knew all the way through on their guitars.

Leroy played *The March of the Wooden Soldiers* from *The Nutcracker Suite* on his cornet, only hitting a couple wrong notes. Everyone was tapping their feet by the end of the song.

The next play was *The Christmas Story*. Carol was the narrator. There were only a few speaking parts so Carol did most of the talking. Billy was Joseph. Marian was Mary. Jimmy was the innkeeper. Roger, John and Gary were the three shepherd boys. Lois was the angel that spoke to the shepherds and Frank, Jake and David, in full costume, were the Three Wise Men.

I don't know what Mrs. Craig was thinking picking Lois as the angel with the biggest speaking part. To me, Lois doesn't look anything like an angel. I think Cora, with the blonde curly hair, should have been the angel. Lois, the angel, was supposed to say:

"Be not afraid
Lo, I bring you tidings of great joy
For onto you is born today in the city of David
A child who is Christ the Lord."

But when poor Lois first spoke, it came out: "B-b-be n-not a-fr-fr-fraid." I felt so sorry for her. I think Mrs. Craig thought Lois just gets nervous, and the more she practiced, the better she would get. But that wasn't how it worked out. She stuttered just as much today as she did the first day she had the part. Mrs. Craig asked Carol to read the part of the angel too, as long as she was narrator. Mrs. Craig gave Lois's shoulders a little squeeze and told her all she had to do was stand on a small step stool with her arms wide open wearing tag board wings and point to the star on the top of the Christmas tree.

I heard Donna whisper to Marian that she hoped Lois could do that without falling off the stool. I hope Lois didn't hear her. Donna is so mean.

We sang more Christmas songs as an entire school and then it was my turn to say the closing poem. Everything went well.

We pushed all the desks to the back of the classroom and set up rows and rows of brown folding chairs stored in the basement. Everything was ready for the performance tonight.

* * *

The ball diamond had been plowed and was already crowded with cars and trucks when our family drove into the school grounds. When we pulled open the front door of the school we were greeted by a rush of warm air and the buzz of voices.

"What a beautiful tree."

"The school doesn't even seem the same."

"Everyone looks so nice."

Cora rushed over to me in a shiny blue dress with a white lacy collar and at least two can-can petticoats making it stick out. She had a matching blue hair ribbon and blue satin shoes. I had a red plaid dress with a black velvet collar and cuffs and tiny black velvet buttons going down the front and matching my black patent leather shoes. My straight brown hair had been washed and set with rags so it formed soft waves around my face. All the boys had on suits and ties or at least dress shirts and ties. Their hair was actually washed and combed and their shoes shined. The girls looked like a beautiful string of Christmas lights with their pretty party dresses of all colors and their curled hair.

Even Mrs. Craig looked special. She had had her hair done at the beauty parlor, and the silver streaks looked classy through the dark of the rest of her hair. She was wearing a wine-colored suit with a brown fake fur collar. Mr. Craig, a heavy-set, bald man with kind looking eyes, stood off to one side because he really didn't know anyone.

No one expected Karla to show up after this morning's accident, but she came, big as life with a lot of her sister's make-up trying to conceal the many scratches and bruises on her face. Karla was wearing a soft pale pink sweater with a gray felt skirt that had a pink fuzzy poodle on one side. She had on real nylons, not long white cotton stockings up to our thighs held up with garter belts like the rest of us. At least the white stockings were prettier than our everyday ugly brown ones.

Everyone rushed over to her. You could see she was loving all the attention by the way she tossed her head and swung her hips so her skirt would flare out. When she smiled the light glittered off a gold tooth her dentist had put in place of the broken one.

At eight o'clock, Mrs. Craig shut off all the lights except for the tree lights and spotlights. The audience quieted and this was our signal to line up for the first songs. This was the first time I felt butterflies in my stomach. What if I made a total fool of myself?

Cora came out first and cleared her throat. Someone in the audience laughed.

"We're so glad
you're here today
to see our wondrous Christmas play.

Grandpa, Grandma
Mom and Dad
Brother, sister, Uncle Tad

We'll sing some songs
Please sing along
We hope you all enjoy it.

Cora bowed, her curls tumbling around. That wasn't planned. Why did she go and do that for? Would I have to bow too?

Everything went smoothly, as if we had practiced it that way.

When it was time for the big kids to do their square dance, Karla took her place beside Ned. The tip of the Christmas tree shook, but the rest of the tree stood firm.

After the solos and duets, it was time for *The Christmas Story*. I saw Lois for the first time that night. She was wearing a white satin and lace dress with thin white cotton stockings and white satin shoes. Her mother had piled her mousy brown hair up on the top of her head with big loopy curls held in place with bobby pins covered with rhinestones. It looked like diamonds were sprinkled throughout her hair. She had on her tag board and gold glitter wings. On her hair was a circlet of gold garland. She looked so beautiful, like what I think a real angel probably looks like. When it was time for the angel to appear, Lois climbed onto the top step of the little ladder, spread her arms and sang the words she was unable to say in practice that afternoon. Everyone couldn't believe their ears when they heard that sweet pure child's voice sounding as angelic as anything could. After she finished, the audience stood up and applauded. I guess Mrs. Craig had picked the best angel of all.

Later after the program, Lois told us how she had felt so bad that Carol would read her part and was crying at home. Her mother told her about a country singer that stuttered when he talked, but could sing without any stuttering. So Lois tried it and sounded so good, her mother dressed her as the angel she really was. I'm so glad for her. I guess she showed that mean Donna.

After the play and the wise men took a different route home, the whole school sang a few more songs together. Then Susan and her friends Dorothy and Carol, with Arlene on the accordion, sang We *Wish You a Merry Christmas* several times with the whole school joining together singing the last time.

It was finally time for my closing poem. I marched to the front of the room and wiped my sweating palms on the front of my new dress. I found my mother in the audience and focused on her pretty face as I recited my poem.

> *"Now it's time to*
> *say good-bye*
> *to friends and family.*
>
> *Music, laughter,*
> *smiles and fun*
> *we pass along to thee.*
>
> *So go enjoy*
> *this Christmas cheer.*
> *We hope it lasts*
> *throughout the year!*

The Christmas program was over but not the best part, the exchange of gifts. We heard a stomping and a jingling of bells in the hallway. It was the jolly fat man himself all the way from the *North* Pole! All the little kids stopped fidgeting and bawling and stood staring in amazement. Santa walked up by Mrs. Craig and sat on a stool she had provided for him. He then proceeded to call off the names on the presents she handed to him. When it was my turn he handed me a small box wrapped in shiny green paper with a gold bow on it. "To: Jean. From: Cora" read the name tag.

Cora was watching me like our cat watches the bird feeder. She was hardly able to control her excitement.

"Cora," I screeched. "You lied to me!"

"I had to," she insisted. "Otherwise, it wouldn't have been a surprise."

Inside was a little jewelry box. Inside the box was half of a Best Friends necklace. Cora was wearing the other half around her neck.

Keith did have Cora's name and gave her a bright green scarf and mitten set. That must have cost a lot more than a dollar. Maybe Keith did have a crush on her. The only problem was, when she got hot, the scarf made her neck turn green.

Gary liked his leather pouch with twenty-five marbles, two shooters and a steely and a cat's eye. He gave Roger back the borrowed steely.

Santa passed out the brown bags filled with fruit, popcorn balls, mixed nuts and candy to the students and brothers and sisters. The Christmas program was over for another year.

Chapter Ten
Gloomy January

Just as December had been snowy and blowy, January brought even more below-zero temperatures and some really sad news.

Mrs. Johnson, Matthew and Mark's mother, had died during Christmas vacation. The twins would not be back the rest of the school year. All the kids were going to live with Grandma and Grandpa for a while in Rhinelander. Grandma Johnson had told Judy's mother that it would be easier for her to take care of them in her big house with Grandpa there to help her. When the baby was a little bigger and Mr. Johnson wasn't so sad, he could probably handle everything again. I would miss Matthew, because he was so nice. I might even miss Mark, although he could be really annoying. Still, they were too young to have something like that happen to them. What if something like that happened in my family?

I don't like January. It's always cold and gray. As far I was concerned, we could just skip right over January and go to February. Cora said, what about all the people who have birthdays in January? I told her they could pick any other month to celebrate their birthday. She said that wouldn't be the same, and it was a goofy idea anyway.

Because of the below-zero temperatures, we were forced to stay inside at recess. This was fun the first few days because Mrs. Craig always made us play outside, whether we wanted to or not. It felt like we were getting away with something.

All the girls had received hula hoops for Christmas, except Cora, Peggy, Cheryl and Sheila, who already each had one. Every recess, the girls went down to the basement and practiced the skill of hula hooping. After a few days. we were pretty good at it. The older girls soon tired of doing the same thing over and over and went upstairs to sit in groups and talk about boys, clothes, make-up, Connie Francis' latest hit, Tab Hunter and other boring things.

Andy, Fred, Ray, Roger, and John played downstairs too. They were playing with a new toy Ray had gotten for Christmas. It was called a Slinky. It was a big silver spring, and Ray put one end in each hand and you could watch the action move from one side of the Slinky to the other. It would even walk down the steps.

Ray set it just right and it would tumble from one step to the next.

Ray let Andy take the Slinky and try to get it to walk down the stairs, but instead it got tangled. Andy tried to untangle it, but it didn't work. Ray quickly grabbed his toy, sat on the steps and tried again to straighten it out. It didn't work. Ray took the slinky and threw it in the trash.

"I'm sorry," Andy mumbled. "Here, buy a new one." He pulled a crumpled five-dollar bill out of his pocket and gave it to Ray.

"Thanks." Ray managed to smile. "You don't have to do that," but he hurriedly took the money and shoved it in his pocket anyway.

Everyone knew Andy had received that money from his Aunt Margaret. Andy must have felt really bad about messing up the Slinky to give Ray his Christmas money.

Andy is probably one of the nicest people you will ever know. Everybody in school liked Andy; even the bullies didn't pick on him. He never said anything bad about anyone. He was a stocky kid with twinkling blue eyes, a spattering of freckles across his nose and blond hair worn in a short spiky crew cut. Every school has a class clown, and Andy was ours. He was the kid who always says something silly when the teacher is trying to be serious. He was constantly showing off. He laughed longer and louder than anyone else at himself. Sometimes he's annoying, but mostly he's funny.

Since the boys couldn't play with the Slinky, they decided to harass the girls. They would walk by while we were hula-hooping and accidentally on purpose bump into the hula hoop to knock it to the floor. Finally, Diane had had it. When John bumped her hoop, she took it and tried throwing it over his head like a lasso. I don't know what she thought she would do with him once she caught him. The rest of the girls started lassoing the boys too. They always got away, but the fun was in the chase. We were having a lot of fun until Cora knocked off Fred's glasses, and one of the lenses fell out. Mrs. Craig was able to put the lens back in, but she put a stop to our fun, by telling us to take our hoops home and leave them there.

We tried jumping rope, but Mrs. Craig complained about the dust thrown up from the floor. Besides, the ceiling wasn't high enough, and the rope kept catching.

By the second week of staying inside every day, my friends and I were bored. There were a few board games like checkers, chess and Scrabble. Since my group was just learning to read, yet alone spell. Scrabble was out. I hated games like checkers and chess where you have to use strategy and think two steps ahead. I always lost.

So Cora, Sandy, Judy and I usually ended up playing Old Maid. Cora is such a bad sport. I would almost rather be the Old Maid myself, then have to put up with her pouting and crabbiness. It's just a game, for goodness sake, not a prediction of the future.

I guess that's why when I saw Cora peeking at my cards I got mad.

"Stop cheating," I demanded. "You're looking at my cards."

"I am not," Cora denied.

"You are, too," I insisted. "I saw you and now you're lying about it. Why do you always have to cheat?"

"Jeannie, how dare you accuse me of cheating!" At this point, we were both shouting and getting looks from other kids. "Did you see me cheating, too?" Cora stared directly at Judy and Sandy.

Sandy wouldn't look at Cora but nodded her head. Judy looked Cora right in the eyes and said, "Yes."

"I guess I know when I'm not wanted." Cora jumped up and walked away a few steps, then turned around and came back.

"Give me my Best Friend necklace back. You're no best friend of mine. Best friends don't call their other best friend liars and cheats."

I was totally shocked but took it off and handed it back to Cora. I didn't bother to point out that it had been a gift and really wasn't hers to take any more.

"Here, take it. I don't want to be best friends with someone who lies and cheats, anyway."

That was a miserable day. Cora and I sat right beside each other in reading class and never said a word to one another. At recess, Cora hung out with Sheila and Darlene. If Cora saw me looking at her, she'd turn her back and say something to her new friends. Then they'd look at me and laugh.

I wondered if she would give one of them the other half of her Best Friends necklace. Maybe they didn't care if she cheated at Old Maid because she was fun to have around. Maybe they were the type of friend that would overlook things like that so they wouldn't break up a great friendship. Maybe they didn't care if they were the Old Maid three times in a row because Cora was looking at their cards. Sandy and Judy were nice, but they were boring and couldn't think of half the fun things to do that Cora did. Maybe I should apologize to Cora for calling her a liar and a cheat, but she was, so I didn't do anything.

This went on for four days. I was miserable. I wondered if Cora was, too. Probably not. Every time I watched her she was laughing with her new friends.

On the fifth day, I was in the girls' coatroom trying to slip off my slacks from under my dress and re-hook my ugly brown right stocking that never stays put. Girls couldn't wear slacks in school, even under their dresses. I tried not taking off my shoes but that didn't work. So I finally had to untie my shoes, slip off the slacks and retie my shoe. I was the last one left in the hall, or so I thought. When I looked up, Cora was standing there waiting for me. I was ready to march right past her without saying a word when she grabbed my arm.

"Jeannie, I'm sorry I cheated and got mad at you. I miss my best friend." She held out my half of the necklace to me.

I suppose I should have made her promise not to cheat at any games any more, but I missed my best friend, too. I just grabbed the necklace, put it on and gave her a big hug.

A few things happened in January which helped break up the endless, cold, gray, dreary days.

Mrs. Craig announced one Monday that we would start taking iodine tablets. Some doctor or someone came up with the idea that America's children weren't getting enough iodine in their diet. We didn't know what iodine was, that's probably why we weren't getting enough. The tablets were enormous, chocolate and hard to chew. Some kids didn't like them, but I didn't mind. Roger liked them so much, that when the teacher wasn't looking, he always begged iodine tablets from other kids who didn't like them. In a few weeks, he probably had enough iodine in his body to last a lifetime.

Another new thing to break up the boredom were duck and cover drills. I guess they had practiced these during World War II, but that was before my time. Mrs. Craig said the school board wanted us to practice these because we were in a cold war with the United Soviet Socialist Republic. School board, my foot. Everyone knew that Fred's dad had dug a bomb shelter behind their farmhouse. Daddy said that the school board gave in because they were fed up with Fred's dad bringing up the same thing every month. The school board felt these drills were better than building a bomb shelter on school grounds. Fred's shelter sounded kind of neat, although I don't know how long I would like being underground. Fred said that their shelter was pretty big and the whole family could fit in it. They had army cots and blankets and all kinds of canned food and water and flashlights and board games and candy. They would poop in a big bucket and these chemicals, you put in, would get rid of it. Fred said that they had enough food and water to last a month, because it would take that long for the radiation to lessen. I didn't have any idea what he was talking about. When I asked Daddy if we were going to build a bomb shelter, he said only when blind horses drove cars. I didn't think that was going to be anytime soon.

Mrs. Craig continued, explaining that we were in a cold war with the Soviet Union. Everyone glanced out the window. It didn't have anything to do with the weather, though. It meant that our armies weren't fighting each other, but the Soviet Union and the United States of America didn't like each other very much and weren't talking to each other. Cora and I looked at each other and grinned. We knew all about that.

She said that the Soviet Union had an atomic bomb, just like the United States did and the fear was that Russia might drop it on our country. The school board (Fred's dad) felt that our school should practice duck and cover drills, just like we practiced fire drills, so if a bomb actually were dropped we would know what to do. Teacher would say "Duck and cover," and we'd all duck and hide under our desks.

Jake wildly waved his arm until Mrs. Craig called on him.

"Jake, do you have a question?"

"Why would they drop a bomb on Tug Lake School?" Jake asked.

"Yeah," Keith said. "Wouldn't it make more sense to drop a bomb on a real big city?"

"What are they going to get here?" Andy interjected. "Cows?" He laughed so hard, I thought he'd split a gut. The other boys laughed, too.

"You're right, children," Mrs. Craig said. "The enemy would probably attack a much larger city, But," and she gave a big sigh, "our school board feels all students should know what to do if the situation came up." She was looking frustrated.

Susan raised her hand. Mrs. Craig nodded at her.

"I've been reading in the paper about how people are building their bomb shelters out of thick cement." Fred was vigorously nodding his head in agreement. "Wouldn't it make more sense to go to the basement, at least? What good will us hiding under our desks do?" Susan wasn't trying to be a smart aleck. She thought she was helping.

Mrs. Craig set her lips in a straight line and repeated that our school board felt it was important that we practice these duck and cover drills.

To stop any further questions, Mrs. Craig shouted, "Duck and cover!"

We all ducked and hid under our desk, or tried to. Leroy was so tall that he could hardly smoosh himself under his desk, and Jimmy was so big that more of him was sticking out than was hidden.

Every day, Andy asked Mrs. Craig if we were going to have a "Quack Quack" drill. That was his name for the duck and cover drills. She would just give him a tight smile, which wasn't much of a smile, more of an annoyed sneer.

Thank goodness, after about a week, Andy got tired of asking, and then, of course, the drill took place. It was in the afternoon, right before recess. The seventh grade had just finished a social studies lesson at the big table and several other kids were at the bubbler for drinks.

Mrs. Craig boomed, "Duck and cover!"

I heard a girl scream. Oh yeah, that was me! Then Sandy and Cora started screaming, too. The boys that were out of their seats made a big show of running into each other and careening off into chairs and desks. Some of the boys who had been at their desks, got up and started belly bumping each other. It was sheer pandemonium. Then we heard Mrs. Craig's loud voice, "One, two, three..." and we knew if we wanted to have recess, we'd better be under our desks and quiet by the time she got to ten.

Poor Leroy cracked his head a good one on the side of his desk, but by the number ten we were all under our desks and quiet. We were supposed to remain quiet for five minutes. The first minute went fine, then we heard a loud fart.

"Jimmy," Andy scolded from under his desk.

"Wasn't me," Jimmy replied.

Then we heard two more farts in quick succession.

"Andy, stop that right now!" Mrs. Craig scolded.

Andy was sitting under his desk making farting noises with his hand stuck in his armpit.

That was the last duck and cover drill we ever practiced at Tug Lake School when I was there. I think Mrs. Craig would rather take her chances with a foreign country than go through that again.

* * *

One frosty January morning, Mrs. Craig greeted us with an announcement that we would all have to go to the town hall to get vaccinations. She passed out cards for our families to fill out and give approval. Teacher said a vaccination was a shot in your arm to prevent some horrible disease. Mrs. Craig said that a little bit of the disease germ was put into your body with a shot in the arm. Then your body would build up armies to fight this disease. So when you actually came in contact with the real germ, you already had armies to fight it inside your body, so you wouldn't get sick.

Most of us would have to get two vaccinations. The older kids would only need a booster shot. One of the shots was for diphtheria and whooping cough. I told Mrs. Craig that I had whooping cough when I was three months old, so my body already had armies built up against that one. She said those two vaccinations came in one shot and I had to get it anyway. The other vaccination was to prevent small pox. I guess small pox is a lot like chicken pox, only a hundred times worse. Whereas chicken pox makes you tired and itches like crazy, small pox could actually kill you.

Everyone started talking. The older kids said that the small pox shot was the worse. The doctor would scratch the skin on your arm, kind of like a tic-tac-toe board and then drop in some of the small pox germ. After about a week, a big scab would form. It was important not to pick at this scab because this was the small pox. Then after about a week, the scab fell off, leaving an ugly scar on your arm. Everyone showed each other their scars.

On the day of the shots, everyone wore short sleeves with sweaters that were easy to remove. We piled on the school bus and headed for the town hall. The parking lot was filled with buses. All the country schools were getting vaccinated.

Cora and I clung to each other. We didn't care who teased us. This was scary stuff.

The town hall was organized chaos. There were doctors in their white coats and nurses with their white uniforms and cute little hats. The place reeked of rubbing alcohol and the noise was deafening. Kids were all over the place. Some were standing in small groups talking or laughing. Some were in long lines waiting for their turn to get the vaccinations. Others were sitting against the wall with their heads shoved between their knees, with nurses hovering around them. Those were the ones that scared me!

We put our coats in a pile on a table that was labeled Tug Lake. Then we were ushered into several different lines depending on the shots you were getting. Cora saw her cousin, Mike, and waved wildly. I looked for my cousin, Helen, but only saw kids that looked as scared as I felt.

When I was almost up to the front of the line, I heard a soft moan in the line next to me and then Andy yelled "Timber!" I saw Leroy crumple to the floor. His legs were all sprawled out and in the way. He looked terribly pale and had a goofy expression on his face. A nurse came and stuck something under his nose. His eyes fluttered open, and he brushed the hand away that was holding the bottle of stinky stuff. Two nurses walked him over to the wall, where he sat down and put his head between his knees.

Then Cora was at the front of the line. She watched the entire time the doctor gave her the two vaccinations. Next it was my turn. The nurse swabbed alcohol on my arm and the doctor quickly stuck in the needle. I looked away. The nurse then turned me around, swabbed my arm and the doctor gave me the small pox shot. This one stung.

I must have looked pale because the nurse kept asking me if I was all right. Of course I was all right, my shots were over!

* * *

It was another below-zero morning before school started, and we were yet again forced to stay inside and play games. Cora, Sandy, Judy and I were playing, "Bird, Beast, or Fish." Judy was it and had just pointed to Cora and yelled fish and started counting to ten. Cora answered, "Cow," then quickly added, "Fish." She was arguing that there was such a thing as a cowfish, when we heard a big bang.

We saw a chair lying on its side by the big table where Andy and James were playing chess. Andy was sprawled on the floor. We turned back to our game, because we figured Andy was showing off again.

We saw people hurrying over to Andy. We looked at each other and went over, too.

Andy was lying on his back on the floor. His whole body was twitching, his eyes had rolled up in his head and drool was coming out of the side of his mouth. I expected him to sit up any minute, give us a goofy grin and brag about how he had really fooled us.

"Quick," Mrs. Craig said, "move the chairs so he won't hurt himself by hitting them. He's having a seizure."

Cora and a few others quickly sprang into action and removed anything he could hurt himself with. Mrs. Craig shoved her sweater under his head to cushion it. Someone gave her a tongue depressor out of the first aid kit and she gently worked it between his clenched teeth so he wouldn't bite his tongue.

I stood there frozen to the spot, unable to think or move. It seemed like the seizure lasted forever, but probably lasted only a few minutes. The twitching stopped, and Andy went into a peaceful sleep. When

Mrs. Craig could see that the worst was over, she called his parents.

Andy had all kinds of tests done. They sounded funny when he told about them, but were probably pretty scary. I know I don't want little wires all over my head. They never found what caused the seizure, and Andy never had another one.

Cora said she wanted to be a nurse when she grows up. I didn't.

Chapter Eleven
Valentine's Day

It was Billy's twelfth birthday. The entire family, even my dad, had spent two hours frosting cupcakes to look like snowmen. The cupcakes were covered with white frosting and sprinkled with coconut. We had put on marshmallow heads with raisin eyes, candy corn noses and cinnamon candy mouths, all held on with frosting.

As Billy passed out his birthday treat to the students and Mrs. Craig. I noticed that he gave the largest cupcake to Marian. She gave him a sweet smile and he actually blushed. I hope he doesn't have a crush on her, of all people.

The entire school sang "Happy Birthday" When everyone stopped singing, Andy continued:

> *"Happy birthday to you*
> *You belong in a zoo.*
> *You look like a monkey*

And you smell like one, too!"

When Andy received his treat, he said. "Say good-bye to your head, Frosty," and he bit off the entire marshmallow in one bite. Sometimes I wonder about him.

* * *

February brought with it bright skies and warmer temperatures, at least above zero. I haven't been to prison, but I imagine the feeling of freedom when they let you out is probably much the same as being allowed to play outside after being kept indoors for a whole month.

We, of course, had to check the playground to see if there were any changes. The snow looked dirty and pretty much trampled down. We needed a fresh snowstorm with some packing snow. In the meantime, we found an ice pond on the side of the school. It wasn't really pond shaped but rather a long strip of sheer blue ice, about five feet wide that ran the entire length of the building. It was the result of melting snow dripping from the roof and refreezing at night. It was just perfect for sliding.

Taking turns, we would run full speed until we hit the ice. Then we slid on our feet as far as possible. The idea was to see who could go the furthest on their feet without falling down. Billy was the best. He could slide the entire length of the building without falling. The rest of us spent a lot of time spinning around on the ice on our backside. Jimmy didn't even bother to try sliding on the ice with his feet. He just plunked down on his backside and slid to the end. Everyone always wanted to take the turn behind Jimmy, because the ice was always cleaned off and you could slide faster. Cora and I sometimes went together. If you held onto your partner's hands and pulled just right, you could turn in circles.

There weren't any windows on this side of the building, so I don't know if Mrs. Craig knew what we were doing. She never said anything. She probably had an idea when kids were coming in with bruises, but no one ever complained for fear that she would ban us from using the ice, just like she banned the hula hoop. One day, I smashed the back of my head so hard that I actually saw red, blue and yellow stars for an instant. I cried. Arlene held an icicle to the spot and it felt better. I didn't tell any adult.

The fun lasted for about a week, until Marian got hurt pretty bad. She was showing off by sliding on one leg with the other leg held up in the air behind her. She was doing good until she hit a twig frozen into the ice. She tripped, and her face hit the ice. She screamed so loud, even Mrs. Craig inside the school heard her and came running. Her sister, Darlene, pushed her way to the front of the crowd that had gathered around Marian. Darlene started crying when she saw all the blood coming from a deep cut in her sister's chin. Her carefully brushed hair was all tangled around her face and she was shaking.

Billy had been the first to reach her. He pressed his clean handkerchief to her chin and helped her hold it. Mrs. Craig put an arm around her on one side and Billy did the same on the other side. Karla tried pushing Billy out of the way, but he would have none of it. There was a trail of blood in the snow that everyone tried to avoid as they all followed Marian into the school.

Marian should have been taken to the doctor because she ended up with quite a scar that never disappeared, but after a phone call to her parents, they gave Mrs. Craig permission to help her. Her parents couldn't come because they were trying to thaw water pipes that went into the barn. Because we were so far from town, no one went to the doctor unless they had something broken or were dying. Mrs. Craig examined Marian's chin and cleaned it with alcohol and put on some kind of reddish liquid that stunk and really hurt, because Marian let out a shriek when Mrs. Craig put it on the cut. Then teacher took tiny strips of medical tape to hold it together. Then she covered it with thick gauze and gave Marian a couple aspirins. I wonder if Mrs. Craig ever thought of being a nurse. She's really good at this.

The next day when we got to school, Marian called to Billy. She had fresh gauze on her chin and both eyes were black and blue. She looked really bad, but I'll give her one thing, she's a tough cookie.

"Billy, wait, I've got something for you. Here, thanks for helping yesterday." She reached into her school bag and pulled out a clean white handkerchief with a thin blue line forming a border around it. "I couldn't get all the stains out of yours, so I took one of my dad's new ones. He'll never know it's gone."

"Geez, you didn't have to do that," Billy squirmed around and his face turned bright red, but he seemed pleased at the same time.

"I wanted to," she smiled sweetly at him.

"How are you feeling? Maybe you should have stayed home today?"

"I know, but I wanted to see you." She smiled. "To return the handkerchief," she hurriedly added.

Oh, for crying out loud, I thought. *Is this mushy stuff going on forever?*

"Billy, come on," I tugged at his jacket. "We're missing all the fun!"

"Go on without me, Squirt. I'll be right there."

"Fine, but you're missing all the fun," I shouted over my shoulder. I don't think Billy even heard me. He was too busy gazing into Marian's green eyes and laughing at something stupid she had just said.

I forgot all about Billy and Marian when I reached the ice pond. Everyone was standing around talking. Mrs. Craig had struck again! Sand was spread all over the ice.

We turned to "Kick the Can." Diane had brought a coffee can a while ago, and we used that. I'm not a fast runner, so I don't like to be It. Everyone always kicks the can before I can get there and count them out. So we are always starting over. Usually after a few times, Billy will take my place as It. Today, though he was busy talking to dumb old Marian, and I was It all recess!

Mrs. Craig had the back tables covered with sheets of plastic and had piles of newspapers the sixth and seventh graders had been bringing since Thanksgiving. On the plastic sheets, there also were pans of blue liquid. She called the sixth and seventh grades back to the table and gave them each a smock, but they really were old dress shirts from her husband.

"We're going to make Papier-Mache globes."

Each student was given a round balloon to blow up and tie with a long string. Of course, dumb old Marian couldn't blow up her balloon because it hurt her chin, so Billy blew hers up for her. Next, they tore off strips of newspaper and dragged it through the blue starch. (Starch dries really hard. My mother uses it for the collars and cuffs of my dad's dress shirts to keep them from getting wrinkly when he sweats during the day.) The kids wrapped the strips around the balloon and tore smaller strips to make lumps, which were supposed to be continents.

All the kids at their desks kept turning around to see what was going on. Mrs. Craig didn't mind as long as you did some work in between peeks. The bigger kids always got to do the fun things.

The paper covered balloons were hung on a wire in the basement to dry. It took about a week.

Then they painted them. Blue oceans, green lands and Antarctica was white. Some of them had used way too much starch, and their continents had slid south. All Andy's continents were down by Antarctica. They hung them in the basement again for a week before they printed the names on with old-fashioned ink pens. Billy said his hands were too big to write nicely, so Marian printed his names for him. Oh, brother!

Some of the globes looked really nice.

When they were able to take them home, Andy broke his in half and wore it as a football helmet.

* * *

One day, Ned brought in a tissue box stuffed with shredded tissue. He wouldn't show anyone, even Susan, until he went in the school. He pulled away the tissue, and all tangled in one corner were six tiny baby mice. They had black, beady eyes and gray fur with long tails.

"I found 'em in the tool shed behind a stack of lumber, just a-squealing. Our cat musta got the mother. My pa said to get rid of them." Ned looked embarrassed, probably because he was a softy and because he hadn't done what his dad had told him to do, because he liked all kind of animals, even scaly ones. "I thought y'all might like to see before I let them go in the woods. They like grain."

He fished in his jacket pocket and produced a handful of oats. The baby mice didn't move from their tangled sleep. Then Ned reached in and handed a baby to my big sister. She looked like that was the greatest gift she had ever received. Then Billy handed one to Marian. All the other girls were making cooing sounds and comments about their tiny little soft ears. I just stood in the background watching. I don't like mice. They carry germs and chew the buttons off your favorite shirt when you forget to hang it up one night and leave it on the floor. I think it's the tail that bothers me. They remind me of snakes. I hate snakes.

The next recess, the girls rushed over to the darling baby mice.

"One's missing," Arlene observed.

Sure enough, instead of six gray little mice huddled together in the corner of the box, there were only five. We spent the rest of the recess looking for that little guy, but couldn't find him. I could tell Mrs. Craig wasn't too thrilled by the prospect of a loose mouse. I think she felt the same way as I did about mice. She couldn't very well set out traps because the girls thought of them as pets. Everything was fine until arithmetic class when Marian let out a scream and started jumping around like she had ants in her pants. Actually, she had a mouse in her pocket. The little guy must have climbed in there to get away from the people and take a nap. After he woke up, he started climbing around, and that's what had freaked Marian out.

How stupid could you get not knowing you had a mouse in your pocket?

* * *

Valentine's Day was coming. Teacher said it was important to give everyone a card, not just your good friends. You didn't have to like someone to be kind. So I guessed I'd give dumb old Marian a card. I thought of drawing a rat on her card, but she'd probably think it was a mouse and say the card was "darling."

"You're just jealous," Cora stated. "Billy is paying more attention to her than you, and you don't know how to take it."

"I am not jealous," I said. "She's mean, just like Karla and Donna."

"No, she's not," insisted Cora. "Everyone thinks she's as bad as those other two, but she really isn't. Name one mean thing she's done."

I couldn't think of anything.

"See," said Cora. "Now think of something mean that Karla or Donna did."

I could think of plenty.

"I don't care. If you hang around jerks, you're a jerk." I turned and walked away.

Mrs. Craig had set out piles of pink, red, white and pastel colored construction paper. Everyone was busy making valentines when they were finished with their schoolwork. Gary was using the new art supplies he had won at Christmas and was drawing a little picture on each of the small white hearts he had cut out. Most of us, though, were cutting out hearts of different colors and pasting them on folded pieces of construction paper to look like fancy Valentine cards in the stores. I and no one else in school had ever received one of those. They cost a lot of money, twenty-five cents. Only adults gave each other store-bought cards. Mrs. Craig printed some valentine words and phrases on the chalkboard that we could copy. I printed "Happy Valentime's Day" inside each card.

When I was making Marian's card, I thought of my brilliant plan. I would make a simply gorgeous card and write Marian's name on it, but not sign it. She'd think some other boy liked her and leave Billy alone, or maybe Billy would get jealous and leave her alone. Anyway, the end result would be that they would no longer like each other.

I couldn't work on it at school because someone might see me. I didn't tell Cora because she wouldn't agree with me. So I sneaked some pink and white paper home to work on the card there. I folded the pink paper into a card shape and pasted on the white paper. I had folded and refolded the white paper, cutting it like a snowflake with a million tiny holes, so it looked real fancy. I pasted a small pink heart in the center and sprinkled silver glitter all over the front of the card. Inside the card, I asked my mother to print "Be My Valentine." I didn't want anyone to recognize my handwriting. I told my mom it was a card for Mrs. Craig.

The day of the party, everyone was wearing red or pink, even Mrs. Craig. We all put our cards into a large cardboard Valentine box that the eighth grade girls had decorated to look like a gingerbread house with heart shaped windows and little red hearts to look like bricks on the chimney. We didn't learn much that day. We kept looking at the wax paper covered containers of cookies, cupcakes and sandwiches sitting on the back table and thinking about the pop cooling in the wash tub. At last, it was party time. The lunch was served and then the eighth graders got the job of passing out the valentines.

We all started reading our cards. My valentine from Gary had a mother and baby chickadee sitting on a branch with tiny red berries on it. How did Gary know I loved birds? Cora's card from Gary had a fuzzy gray kitten on it.

My card from Roger had a little heart on folded paper, so when you opened the card, the heart popped out. On the heart, he had printed "Happy Heart Day."

Sandy's card to me said, "happy valentine bay."

Cora's card had two touching hearts that said, "Friends Forever."

I heard Marian squeal as she pulled a store-bought card from her pile. She opened the pure white envelope. Inside the envelope was a shiny white card with a beautiful red rose on the front. Inside the card it said, "Have a beautiful Valentine's Day" and was signed "Billy." *That card must have cost thirty cents at least! What was he thinking?*

Marian turned and gave Billy a toothy smile and said "Thanks." You could see how pleased she was. Billy seemed a little flustered, because at that point he accidentally knocked his pile of cards to the floor.

Then Marian pulled out the card I had made for her. "It's gorgeous," she said.

"Somebody really likes you," Karla giggled, looking at Billy with a smirk on her face.

"Open it," Donna prompted.

"That's strange," Marian said, looking at the inside of the card. "There's no name that tells who it's from."

"You must have a secret admirer," Karla tittered wickedly.

"I don't care," Marian said. "I don't want any admirer who doesn't even have sense enough to sign their name." She took my gorgeous card that I had spent hours making and threw it in the garbage can.

Billy gave her a big grin, and she picked up the card he gave her and held it to her heart. *Yuck!*

I heard Susan say, "Thank you, Billy." She was proudly holding up a red and white store-bought card that said on the front, "To a Great Sister."

I quickly sorted through my pile of cards and there it was. A shiny white store-bought envelope peeked out from beneath the pile of homemade cards. I ripped it open. On the front was a picture of a big boy and a little girl playing with puppies. Inside it said, "To my best friend. Happy Valentine's Day" and signed "Billy."

Chapter Twelve
Judy's Sick

"Mrs. Craig! Mrs. Craig!" I whispered, tapping her on the shoulder as she was working with the fourth grade. One of Mrs. Craig's rules was not to bother her when she was working with a group.

She turned around with a scowl on her face, but she could see how scared I was.

"Judy's really sick, teacher."

She jumped up and told the group to take turns reading paragraphs.

Judy sat in the desk next to me, but today she wasn't sitting. Her head was resting on her arms and her long brown hair was tumbled in a big mess on her desk.

Mrs. Craig gently brushed away the hair and held the back of her hand to Judy's red cheek. Worried wrinkles formed on the teacher's forehead. "Jean, please bring me the thermometer, gauze and rubbing alcohol." She slipped the thermometer between Judy's dry cracked lips. "Keep this under your tongue."

Judy didn't even open her eyes. After three minutes, Mrs. Craig checked the thermometer. Her eyes were enormous when she saw the temperature. She shook down the thermometer and put it back under Judy's tongue. This time, when Mrs. Craig checked the thermometer, her eyes got even bigger.

"Judy, I'm calling your parents," she said and quickly went to the phone.

I kept brushing Judy's hair off her hot face until Mrs. Craig came back.

"Judy, no one answers," she said when she returned. "Do you know where they are?"

"Barn," Judy croaked.

Mrs. Craig went into the storage room and came back carrying an army cot, a blanket and her coat. She set up the cot in the library corner, laid the blanket over it and folded up her coat to use as a pillow. Then Mrs. Craig and I led Judy over to the cot. Mrs. Craig gave Judy two aspirins and a glass of water and made her finish the glass. She went into the kitchen and returned with a dishpan of cold water and a rag. She put the rag in the cold water, rang it out and laid it on Judy's head.

"We're going to try and get your temperature down," Mrs. Craig told Judy, but I don't know if Judy was even listening. "Does anything else hurt?"

Slowly, Judy opened her eyes, but they looked all glassy. "Stiff neck, sore throat, headache," she mumbled. "Belly aches, legs on fire." Two tears sneaked out from under her eyelids and ran down her burning cheeks.

"You just rest, dear," Mrs. Craig whispered to Judy. She turned to me. "Jeannie, we need a big bowl from the kitchen in case she vomits."

When I came back, Mrs. Craig was wringing out the cold rag again and placing it on Judy's forehead. "Jean, keep putting cold cloths on her head. When the water is no longer cold, get cold water from the kitchen. You'll be like Florence Nightingale on the battlefield helping the wounded." She gave me a kind pat on the shoulder, then rushed away.

Why me? I'm not the one who wants to be the nurse. One look at Judy, though, stopped me from feeling sorry for myself.

The other kids were watching me, wishing they could be helping Judy instead of doing schoolwork. In fact, Karla had gone over to Mrs. Craig and asked if she could take my place. Mrs. Craig waved her away like the pesky gnat she is.

I had refilled the dishpan twice by the time Mrs. Craig came back. She had reached Judy's parents and told me to get her school bag and outdoor clothes. When Judy's parents came Mrs. Craig took them aside and whispered to them. We couldn't hear what was being said but they looked really serious.

That recess, no one played. We just stood around and discussed Judy.

"She's really sick."

"I hope I don't get it."

Among all the chatter, Karla's voice rang out. "What if she has polio?"

"Polio, what's polio?"

Karla puffed herself up, like a bird on a fence in winter. She loved being the center of attention. "Polio is a virus that attacks the muscles in the body and paralyzes them, so you can't walk."

"Judy could walk," Andy interjected.

"Right now, yes," Karla said. "But as the polio progresses, it affects more and more of the body. Sometimes they die. I have a cousin that attends North Star School, and he said that a first grader died from polio." She smirked at Cora and me, because we were first graders.

Susan interrupted, "Karla's right, but it just doesn't affect little kids. I saw a report on the news that talked about how President Franklin Roosevelt had polio and couldn't walk. That's why, in pictures, you always see him sitting or just head shots because they would tie him to the speakers' stand when he gave speeches, so he would appear strong."

"My cousin said the whole school was given that new polio vaccine, and no one else got it yet." Karla interrupted, trying to get all the attention again. "Sometimes it paralyzes the lungs and they put the person in a big tin can like thing that breathes for them. Just their head and feet stick out."

"Shut up, Karla," Andy screamed, "or I'll personally put you in a tin can and seal it and throw it in the dump!"

Everyone turned to stare at Andy. This outburst was so unlike him that everyone stopped talking and just looked at him. He was obviously upset because his face was red and he looked like he was going to cry.

Just then, the bell rang calling us into school. No one talked about Judy or polio anymore in a big group, but that's pretty much what everyone whispered about in their small groups at recess for the next few days.

Judy didn't come to school the rest of the week. We heard that no one knew what exactly was wrong with Judy, but she was so sick that she had been taken to a big Milwaukee hospital by ambulance and that her parents and sister were all there with her. Judy's Uncle Harry and Aunt Blanche's family were helping out with the farm chores on Judy's farm while they were gone.

On Monday, a serious looking Mrs. Craig stood behind her desk until we settled down. She stood up there wringing her hands.

"Students, I have some news about Judy. She has polio. Polio is a virus that affects people, mostly children and young adults by paralyzing their arms, legs and lungs. They could die or be left crippled. Some even spend the rest of their life in an iron lung, which is a big machine that looks like a tin can. Only their head sticks out because the machine breathes for them because their own lungs are paralyzed and can't work."

Karla smirked and turned in her chair so everyone could see her. I wouldn't have been surprised if she took a bow.

No one said a word, not even Andy could make this situation funny. I felt tears come to my eyes and I heard others sniffling.

Roger raised his hand. Mrs. Craig nodded at him.

"Is Judy going to die?"

We had all been thinking the same thing, but everyone had been afraid to say it out loud.

Mrs. Craig shook her head. "Judy is not going to die, but she has been very sick. The good news is that her lungs and arms are not affected, but her legs are paralyzed and the muscles are damaged. She will never be able to run or jump again."

I could not even begin to imagine not being able to run or jump. That's what we did every recess. This wasn't fair. How could something so rotten happen to someone so nice?

Mrs. Craig continued, "Judy won't be able to come to school the rest of this year. She will be moved from this hospital to a rehabilitation center where she will learn to walk again with the help of braces and crutches. She will probably be there all summer, but next fall, hopefully, she'll be back in school." Mrs. Craig smiled, but the smile looked forced.

Dorothy raised her hand, "Is she in pain?"

"Yes," Mrs. Craig responded. "Her mother said that the nurses have to put moist hot packs on her legs to keep them from having spasms, which is very painful."

"What are spasms?" Frank asked.

"That's when the muscles in the legs jerk without us being able to stop them." Mrs. Craig replied.

"How did she get polio?" Carol asked.

Mrs. Craig sighed. "The doctors aren't really sure how polio is spread. They think one person gives it to the next person. They don't know if it's through breathing the same air or touch. The doctor thinks Judy might have acquired the virus from her cousin. He had flu-like symptoms when his family visited last month. Most people who get the polio virus don't get really sick like Judy, they just have flu-like symptoms for a few days. Then they're fine. The doctor thinks her cousin had the virus because there was a girl in his school that came down with polio."

"Could we get polio, too?" I had to know.

"Yes, we could," Mrs. Craig said. "We've all been exposed to the virus, but," she hurriedly continued after seeing the looks on our faces, "a scientist named Dr. Jonas Salk has developed a vaccine that can prevent polio. That is why a team of doctors and nurses will be coming to school today to give us all the polio vaccine. Your families have all been contacted and will be coming to school to receive the vaccine also."

At just the mention of getting the polio vaccine, Leroy looked like he was going to faint. Maybe he could sit on the floor to begin with, so he wouldn't have so far to fall.

Mrs. Craig continued, "Judy's family plans on visiting her every weekend. She's pretty lonesome so far away from home. I think it would be nice to write cards and letters to her that her family can deliver."

We all gladly got to work writing letters or making get well cards. At least we were doing something for Judy. I kept thinking of those little boys and girls I had seen on posters to give money for polio research. They always had big smiles as they stood there with big black braces on their legs, leaning on wooden crutches. I wondered why they were smiling. I didn't think I'd be smiling if that terrible thing happened to me.

At recess, all the kids stood in little groups talking about Judy and polio. No one felt like running and jumping around that day. I was over by the swings talking to Sandy and Cora. We were talking about how terrible it would be not to be able to move your legs, when Karla, Marian and Donna strolled over to us.

"Jeannie, you're going to be the next one to get polio, you know," Karla grinned wickedly. "You were helping Mrs. Craig take care of Judy, and Judy breathed right in your face."

I started to cry, and Sandy and Cora both put their arms around me.

"Karla, what a mean thing to say!" Marian stood in front of her cousin and stared her right in the face. "Everyone has just as much a chance of getting polio as Jean does. We've all been exposed to the virus. You didn't need to scare her. Pick on someone your own age." Marian managed to separate my friends so she could put her arm around me and lead me away from Karla. Cora and Sandy trailed along.

"Marian, wait!" Donna called as she ran to catch up with us, leaving a puzzled looking Karla standing by herself, wondering what had just happened.

When we were away from Karla, Marian brushed my hair back from my face and wiped my tears with a pretty lacy handkerchief that smelled of Evening in Paris perfume. "Don't worry, Jeannie. You're not going to get polio. We'll get the vaccine today and everyone will be fine." She smiled at me and looked so pretty, I could see why Billy had a crush on her. Maybe Cora was right; Marian was nice.

After dinner, families started arriving. The little kids were fussy and everyone else looked pretty nervous. The medical team arrived carrying in large metal containers. They arranged us into lines with our families. Sandy's family was a line all by themselves. Leroy was beginning to break out in a cold sweat. Imagine the relief when they brought out the oral vaccine! We were each given a small paper cup with a sugar cube that had a bright pink spot on the top. I guess that pink spot was the virus. I didn't know viruses were that pretty. All we had to do was crunch down the sugar cube. I think all vaccinations should be given that way!

* * *

Mrs. Craig had a big smile on her face and was holding up a piece of blue lined paper. "Students, we have a letter from Judy." Everyone cheered and clapped.

Mrs. Craig read:

"Dear Tug Lake School,

I really miss everyone. Thank you for your cards and letters. I have them tapped on the walls of my room and look at them all the time. I tell anyone who will listen, all about each one of you. Sorry I can't write each one of you a letter, but you know I don't like writing.

I have school two hours a day with a special tutor. Her name is Mrs. Alden. She's not as crabby as Mrs. Craig, but she doesn't have to put up with as many crazy kids as Mrs. Craig does either. The rest of the day I do therapies and rest. When I rest, I've been reading 'The Little House in the Big Woods' series by Laura Ingalls Wilder. I'm on the second book, 'Little House on the Prairie.' They're really good but they make me hungry.

Someone is always messing with me. I need a nurse to do exercises with my legs so they don't shrivel up. I even do exercises in the pool, otherwise my legs just float behind me. Mr. Kramer is helping me to learn to crawl and walk. Right now he moves my legs, but someday I'll do it by myself with the help of braces and crutches.

I've met some new friends, but I won't forget you guys. At night, we kids get to go into the day room and play board games or watch TV. Our favorite show is 'I Love Lucy.' Last Monday, she was working at a candy factory with her best friend, Ethel. They were putting candy in boxes and the conveyor belt started moving so fast they couldn't keep up and the button didn't work to stop the machine. So Lucy was stuffing the candy in her mouth and down her shirt. It was so funny we laughed until tears were coming down our cheeks and we almost wet our pants.

This is a really long letter, so Mrs. Alden said I can stop now. Please come visit me.

Miss you,
Judy"

* * *

"We're going on a field trip," Mrs. Craig announced.

We all looked toward the window. It was pretty cold and snowy to go walking in the woods, but as usual, we were ready for anything.

"The last field trip," John announced, "Cora and Jean got lost and Roger had to find them."

Cora and I turned several shades of red. John can't remember anything, but he remembered that.

Mrs. Craig looked at us kindly and smiled. "Hopefully, no one will get lost on this trip. Next week, Thursday, we're going to Milwaukee to visit Judy at the hospital, then we'll go to the Milwaukee Zoo."

Everyone cheered and clapped. Andy even let out a loud whoop, but Mrs. Craig didn't say anything. She just stood there, smiling.

* * *

It was dark as the school bus pulled out of the schoolyard headed for Milwaukee. We were crammed two or three in a seat, and no one was very comfortable, but we were so excited that no one cared. As soon as it got light, kids were reading or playing Cat's Cradle. No matter how many times the big girls explained it (and showed us), Cora and I still couldn't get it, but it really didn't matter because it made the trip go faster.

When we got near Milwaukee, everyone was staring out the windows at the sky. The beautiful blue sky was now gray. Mrs. Craig explained that the grayness was caused by factory smoke because they burned coal. I had been to Milwaukee several times to see Uncle Gustav and Aunt Louisa, but most of the kids had never left Merrill or gotten any further than Wausau. They were busy pointing out things. It was exciting to see the really tall buildings. Factories were pouring out thick, black smoke from their smokestacks. Houses side by side all exactly the same, with no lawns and few trees.

I don't know if I could find my way home with those look-alike houses. I never want to live in a big city, but Sandy and Cora thought it would be exciting.

The rehabilitation hospital was a big, red brick building with a big parking lot filled with cars. There were lots of windows and there were ramps leading to the front doors. Inside, we caught glimpses of little kids being pushed in chairs with wheels.

The hospital must have known we were coming. We were greeted by a tall woman wearing a starched white uniform with a starched white cap perched on her brown curls.

"You must be Tug Lake School," she said, shaking hands with Mrs. Craig and the other adults. "I'm Mrs. Fowler, one of the many nurses that work with Judy. Judy's missed you all so much. We're so glad you came today." She smiled at us. "Judy is waiting for you in the day room on the second floor. Her room is too small to fit everyone, so we thought you could talk to her there. The elevator can only hold ten, so we'll have to make several trips."

She pushed a big button on the wall that lit up and had an arrow on it pointing up. A metal door slid into the wall and we were looking into a metal room. Everyone held back until several adults started ushering kids into the elevator. Mrs. Fowler got in with them and pushed a button inside the elevator. The door slammed shut. We heard a whirring sound and watched a needle at the top of the elevator move from "G" to "1" to "2" and stop.

After a few seconds the needle came back to "G." The door flew open and Mrs. Fowler was standing alone. This time everyone rushed to get on. When Cora and I finally got our turn, we held each other's hand. It was so crowded that Lois' dad had his elbow stuck right in my face. The door slammed shut, and I felt the elevator rising. I thought my knees would give out, and I'd land on the floor. The elevator came to a shivering halt, and my stomach jumped right into my throat. That was so much fun, I can't wait until we go downstairs. When the door flung open the rest of the school was in a big group waiting for us. It was really quiet, even the school kids were whispering.

When everyone was on the second floor, Mrs. Fowler led the group down the hall. She stopped in front of a door that looked like the other ten doors we had just passed. It said "216" on a shiny sign. Mrs. Fowler said this was Judy's room. We all took turns looking inside.

It was a small room with yellow walls and a high hospital bed with white sheets tightly tucked in under the mattress. A pink teddy bear, without a ribbon, was propped up on the pillow. There was a small nightstand with a tall bottle of lotion and a gray plastic pitcher and a glass of water with a straw. There was a plastic covered chair. The window had yellow curtains pulled to the side. No wonder Judy got lonely.

On the other side were two doors. One I figured was a closet and the other turned out to be her own bathroom. But the neat thing was the dozens of pictures and letters taped to the walls and doors. I found a few of mine.

"This is the day room," Mrs. Fowler announced. "There's Judy waiting for you."

She pointed to the middle of this bright room and there sat Judy in a stiff plastic chair, waving wildly at us. It was Judy, but a new Judy, a Judy who had polio.

We all swarmed around Judy, then stood stiffly not knowing what to say. Judy sat shyly, grinning from east to west, as my dad would say. She was pretty. Her brown hair was done up in ringlets all over her head. She wore a bright red dress, with a lace yoke and a tiny black ribbon at her throat. A thin strip of lace encircled the skirt. On her feet were thick white ugly leather tie shoes that went halfway up her legs. On both sides of the shoes were steal and leather braces that disappeared under her skirt. A pair of clumsy-looking crutches leaned against the chair and a wheelchair was a short way off.

Standing beside Judy was a tall, dark-skinned woman with sparkling brown eyes and bright white teeth. She was also wearing a white uniform and a starched white cap on her short black curls. I had never seen a Negro before, except on TV and she didn't look anything like Sammy Davis Junior.

Mrs. Craig and a few of the adults went up and hugged Judy, but the rest of us hung back, unusually quiet for us.

"Aren't you going to introduce me?" her nurse asked.

Judy giggled, "Tug Lake School, this is Rosie. Rosie, this is Tug Lake School."

"Hi, Tug Lake School," Rosie said in a loud, booming voice.

"Hi, Rosie," we echoed back.

"Judy and I have talked a lot about her Tug Lake friends when I have the night shift and she can't sleep. Who's the artist that drew that pretty picture of a little girl with her kitten?"

"That's Gary!" we all shouted. Gary bashfully raised his hand.

"Where's the boy who always turns on the music program and sounds like an angel?"

"Roger!" we all shouted.

"What?" he answered. We all laughed, including Judy and the nurses. Roger had been taken by surprise. He had been gently rolling the wheelchair back and forth, seeing how it worked.

"Who's the little girl that's the best jump roper in school?" That was me.

Rosie knew something good about every kid in Tug Lake School and even Mrs. Craig. It was obvious that Judy missed us a lot and talked about us all. After the introductions, everyone was talking to each other. We weren't shy anymore.

Judy told us how scary the first days were when she found out about her legs being paralyzed, about her therapies and how hard it was for her to put on the shoes with the braces. They made her do it herself to be more independent, but it took a long time and sometimes she cried before they would help her. I thought that was mean.

We, in turn, explained how we made atoms using tiny little marshmallows and toothpicks, what games we were playing at recess and who had crushes on who.

During all this talking, Jimmy naturally plunked down in Judy's wheelchair, and Andy started wheeling him around the room. We were waiting for Mrs. Craig or the nurses to tell them to stop. When it didn't happen, we all took turns pushing and riding in the wheelchair, too. Frank took her crutches and tried walking with them. It was especially funny to watch tall Leroy trying to use those tiny crutches. Judy and Rosie laughed so hard, tears were running down their cheeks. I knew there would be a lot more talk about the students of Tug Lake School late at night when Judy's legs hurt so bad she couldn't sleep.

Then other nurses brought in the other polio victims and introduced them to us one by one. Gary was especially interested in a teenage girl named Becky, who was paralyzed in both her arms and legs and drew really detailed pictures with a pencil in her mouth. For weeks following the visit, Gary always had a pencil between his teeth trying to draw like Becky, but he finally gave up. Then the nurses passed out over-sized sugar cookies and lemonade. It was like a party.

Cora and I were playing Cat's Cradle with Judy, she knew how to play and helped us a lot, until Mrs. Craig said it was time to leave because we still had to go to the zoo.

"I wish I could go," Judy said.

"Next time," Andy said. "I'll even push the wheelchair." He gave an evil grin and wrung his hands like a mad scientist. Everyone laughed.

It was hard leaving Judy. I looked back as I was leaving the room and saw Rosie and Judy laughing so hard they were both shaking.

Back on the bus everyone was talking like crazy. The older kids started talking about how nice Rosie was and then the talk changed to Negroes. I wasn't the only one who hadn't seen a live Negro. It turns out only the adults and Ned had seen any. Ned had lived in Tennessee, and there were a lot of Negroes there. Ned said there was segregation in the South. That meant that the Negroes couldn't go to the same schools as the white kids, or use the same bathrooms, water fountains, or go to the same restaurants. There were signs that said "White" or "Colored." He said when they rode a bus, the whites were in the front and the Negroes in the back.

One day a Negro woman wouldn't give up her seat to a white man on a crowded bus in Georgia. The police came and arrested her and took her to jail.

Everyone gasped at the thought of being dragged off a bus because you were the wrong color.

Ned continued, "A Negro preacher called Martin Luther King organized a boycott, which meant that the Negroes agreed not to ride the bus until they could sit anywhere. This went on for a year until the bus company was going broke and agreed to let the Negroes ride."

At that point, Frank couldn't take being quiet anymore and said, "Boy, I bet the Negroes and whites really have some fights. If anyone ever tried to get me out of my bus seat, I'd knock their teeth out." He looked around him, as if waiting for someone to try.

"No, that's just it," Ned said excitedly. "That King guy preaches peace. When the police come to arrest them, they're not to fight back. Also, there's a group called the Ku Klux Klan, KKK, that runs around at night wearing sheets and hoods and burning crosses in front of Negro homes."

"Why?" someone asked.

"To scare them."

"Does it work?"

"It would for me!" someone else shouted.

"That's really dumb," Frank commented. "Is that all the KKK does, run around in sheets and burn crosses?"

"Oh no," Ned continued. "They..."

At that moment we heard a sharp," Ned!" and saw Mrs. Craig shaking her head and pointing at all us little kids, who were, of course, all ears.

Then Ned started talking about his Negro friend, Moe, who he fishes with and can spit five feet if he can spit an inch. Mrs. Craig seemed to relax as she turned around in her seat again.

The zoo was nice, but not as nice as seeing Judy. The best part of the zoo was when we saw this big silver gorilla named Sampson. Andy was in front of the glass of the cage pounding his chest and making monkey noises, when Sampson jumped down from the tire swing and started doing the same thing. I thought Andy would pee his pants. Wait 'til I tell Judy.

Chapter Thirteen
The Storm of the Century

The weather man had said there was a chance of snow. I guess he was right, because by nine o'clock in the morning, we already had five inches and no letup in sight. In fact, the snow was starting to come down harder and the wind was picking up. By ten o'clock, we had two more inches and a cold wind was starting to whip the accumulated snow around.

March had come in like a lamb, so it was only right that March would go out like a lion. The winter's snowbanks had shrunk to dirty little mounds sticking up alongside the roads. I, for one, was ready for spring. I was tired of the cold and snow, but my dad kept saying, there's always one good snowstorm in March. Since we hadn't had much snow in March, I guess this was the "one good snowstorm."

We went out for recess, but the cold wind blowing the snow in our faces was miserable. We all came in early. Mrs. Craig didn't say a word. She looked worried. She was waiting for a phone call, or the school bus to show up. At ten-thirty, the much awaited call came. School was being let out early due to the storm. Everyone cheered. The first bus load left, and fifteen of us still remained. We got all bundled up and waited for the bus to come back.

Ned was ready to set off walking to his house when there was a knock on the inner door and the "abominable snowman" appeared. Actually, it was Ned's dad, but he was covered with snow. He stomped his boots on the wooden floor, dropping a ton of snow, which was quickly melting and leaving a puddle around his feet. He unwrapped his long knit scarf and took off his leather cap with fleece-lined ear flaps.

"Sorry to disturb you, ma'am," he fidgeted with the cap in his hands. He looked like an older version of Ned. "I best be taking my boy now. Don't want him walkin' in this storm. I can still get through the woods with the tractor, so I thought I better get him whilst the road's still passable. Won't be for long. Seems like the snow is blowin' every direction but down. You best be takin' these young'uns home before y'all get snowed in."

We looked at each other. We hadn't thought of that! It sounded like fun, until we realized that we'd be without our families, food and comfy beds. No thanks, we'd wait for the bus.

"You're right, Mr. Gedding, these children should be leaving shortly. The bus left a little while ago to take the students home who live on the northern route and should be back soon to take the rest."

"Mrs. Craig, if you think you can't drive home in this blizzard, I'll come back with my tractor and you can hunker in with my family."

None of us could imagine Mrs. Craig riding on a tractor and hunkering anywhere, let alone a logger's shack. Junior let out a laugh, but after Mrs. Craig gave him a dirty look, he put his mitten in his mouth to muffle the sound, but his shoulders kept shaking.

"Thank you, Mr. Gedding, that's really nice of you, but I have to wait until these children leave on the bus. I'll be fine."

"All right, ma'am, good luck! Don't wait too long, it's gettin' worser every minute. Come on, son, we best be goin' whilst we can."

Then as quickly as Mr. Gedding came, he left with Ned, leaving the building feeling more empty and unsafe than before.

It was now eleven-thirty, and two more inches had piled up. The wind was worse, and there was starting to be "white out" conditions, which meant the wind was blowing so hard we couldn't see anything out the window except whirling snow.

"Did he forget us?" Sandy whimpered.

"Of course not," Mrs. Craig snapped, a little too harshly. Then more kindly, she said, "The bus just has to go really slow because of the conditions of the road and the blowing snow. The bus should be here any minute." She didn't sound quite as confident as she had when she talked to Ned's dad.

We had taken off our outside clothes except for our snow pants and boots. We were all gathered around the radio listening to the school closings and the worsening road conditions. It seemed all the factories, schools and businesses were closing early, and still we were waiting. At twelve-thirty the phone rang. Mrs. Craig flew across the room.

"Hello... Mrs. Craig... Hello..." there was a lot of static, but we could hear a man's voice booming over the phone wires, even though Mrs. Craig turned her back so we wouldn't hear. We heard just fine.

"Mrs. Craig, this is John Montgomery." He was president of the school board. "The bus ain't coming. Roy (our bus driver) slid off the road after delivering the first load. The bus is up to the rear axle in a ditch by his uncle, Tiny Kretchum. He's holing up there. There's no way we're getting any bus to you in this storm. Besides, the county has called off the road crews. The plows can't keep up with the storm. The roads are impassable and there's white-out conditions. I guess you and the youngsters will be spending the night at Tug Lake School. You should be fine as long as the power holds. If that goes down it could get pretty cold. You call the families that have phones and I'll call the radio station telling your situation. Hopefully, those families without phones will be listening to the radio and know everyone's safe. We'll pick you up tomorrow as soon as the county plows get through."

When Mrs. Craig set down the phone, she turned to speak to us. She put on a cheery, fake smile. "Well, children, that was Mr. Montgomery… You heard, didn't you?"

We all nodded. Sandy started to cry. Gary wrapped his arm around her.

"It's not that bad," Mrs. Craig said briskly. I didn't know if she was trying to convince us or herself. "It'll be an adventure! We'll be safe and warm inside the school during the blizzard."

"Unless the power goes out," Karla said.

"We're not going to worry about that," Mrs. Craig said hurriedly. "We have too much to do. First, we need to call each family, so they know you're safe."

Mrs. Craig talked to each family, then the kids did. Most of us had never spent the night away from our family. I know I hadn't. It made me think of Judy being away from her family and how brave she must be. I didn't feel brave.

After every family that had a phone was notified and Mrs. Craig had called her husband, we heard a public service announcement on the radio. It said that fifteen students and their teacher were snowed in at Tug Lake School. The county sheriff and state patrol warned everyone to stay off the roads and that the students were safe and warm. I guess we were. That cheered everyone up. We were famous. We had been on the news.

Then Mrs. Craig put us to work finding candles, blankets, flashlights, food and anything else we might need just in case the lights went off. It was surprising how much we found, blankets and flashlights from the haunted house and two cots and blankets from the sick room/storage room. We filled up three big kettles with water. It was close to two o'clock by the time we finished.

"I'm hungry," Roger said.

"My goodness, that's right!" Mrs. Craig exclaimed. "We've been so busy. We haven't even had dinner. It would be a good idea to eat half your dinner now and save half for supper."

"That's what we did. The boys were taking this whole adventure thing to heart. They were thoroughly enjoying themselves.

"Do you want seafood?" Andy asked.

"Sure," the rest of the boys answered.

Andy opened his mouth wide, so everyone could see his half-eaten peanut butter sandwich spread over his tongue and teeth.

"I get it!" Junior shouted. "See food! We saw food!" He thought this was so funny that he laughed so hard he started choking. Andy had to pound him on the back to stop. Then the rest of the boys started laughing, too. I thought boys had a strange sense of humor.

After we had finished eating, Mrs. Craig said, "I wish we had more food, children, but we'll just have to make do with what we have."

"You do have more food," Frank said. "Remember those eggs and potatoes you bought from my dad this morning? They're in the trunk of your car."

"You're absolutely right, Frank. I had totally forgotten about them. This morning seems so long ago.

So much has happened!" I knew exactly what Mrs. Craig was talking about. "There's five dozen eggs and a bushel of potatoes, but no one can go out in this blizzard to get them."

"I'll go, Mrs. Craig," Junior volunteered. "I've had to go to the barn in all kinds of weather to do the chores when my dad can't. I'm strong. You can tie a rope around my waist and hang on to it, so I don't wander off in the snow. I can do it."

Junior's real name was Clarence Abraham Schenicki Junior. I don't blame him for wanting to be called Junior. He was a thin, wiry boy. His hair was always cut in a buzz cut. Junior had enormous hands and feet. He kept saying he would have to grow into his hands and feet like a puppy grows into his paws. I guess that means he'll be a big man like his dad when he grows up. Junior was a strong boy, because he had to do most of the work on the farm. His dad liked his liquor too much and was usually passed out by nighttime chores. His mother was sickly. His older brothers had already left the house, and the bunch of younger brothers and sisters were too small to be any help.

Mrs. Craig was shaking her head. "I can't let you do that, Junior. It's too dangerous."

"Mrs. Craig, we don't know how long we'll be here," Junior begged. "You heard yourself what they said on the radio. The storm front is stalled over Wisconsin and this could go on for several days. We've already eaten most of our food and it hasn't even been one day."

Mrs. Craig looked confused, as she looked around the room at all the faces depending on her to make the right decision.

"The storm's only going to get worse," he pleaded. "And we're going to get mighty hungry."

"All right, I guess you can try, but you must be dressed warmly and tied securely to me."

Junior dressed in his outside clothes, then put on Mrs. Craig's long brown coat and tied her scarf over his knit hat. He had his long knit scarf over his face, so that only a small slit showed where his eyes were. It was obvious he had done this before. He looked funny, but no one laughed.

We then tied the jump ropes, which were made out of binder twine, not rope, together, but they would never have reached the car. Carol suggested we use our scarves to tie together and that worked just fine. We took all our long scarves and tied them together to form a long rope. Mrs. Craig securely wound them around Junior's waist and doubled knotted it so it wouldn't come loose. Then she tied the loose end to herself. We all followed them to the enclosed porch.

With Mrs. Craig's car keys clutched firmly in his gloved and mittened hand, Junior slowly pulled open the door. We couldn't see a thing except blowing, swirling, gusting snow. It stung our faces and quickly started forming drifts in the porch. Unhesitatingly, Junior took two steps into the blizzard and disappeared from our sight. The scarf rope grew tight. Then we saw two tugs on the rope. That was the signal for everyone to start pulling in the rope. It seemed like hours, but truthfully was only probably a few minutes, when a struggling shape stumbled through the wall of snow and dropped a huge sack of potatoes at Mrs. Craig's feet. Before Mrs. Craig could stop him, Junior was out the door and disappeared back into the storm. Leroy hoisted the sack of potatoes over one shoulder and carried it into the school. More quickly this time, we felt the tugs and pulled Junior into the porch carrying two brown paper bags. The bags were quickly taken from him and he dropped to the floor. Junior was totally white. Even the little part of his face that showed around his eyes was wet and snow was clinging to his eyebrows and eyelashes.

Mrs. Craig and the older girls untied the scarf rope from around Junior's waist. This wasn't an easy task because the wool had gotten wet and tight. When he was free, the boys stripped off his wet outer clothes. With one arm around Billy's shoulder and the other around Gary's, he was half-dragged, half-carried into the warm classroom. Other kids scooped up the layers of hats, scarves, coats and boots and lay them near the heater vents to dry. The car keys were frozen to his glove, which was kind of lucky, because I think for sure he would have dropped them in the snow. Arlene had made a pot of coffee with some coffee grounds and a percolator she had found in the kitchen. The school smelled good from the coffee. As Junior took small sips of the burning hot coffee, his teeth finally stopped chattering and his body shaking. He managed a small grin.

"It sure is windy out there," he said. "If I wouldn't have been tied down, I might have taken off like a kite."

Everyone laughed, but we all knew what a brave thing Junior had done. Most of the boys thought this whole situation was fun and exciting, but I think most of the girls were scared like me, only they didn't show it.

One of the brown bags contained five dozen eggs. The other brown bag contained Mrs. Craig's emergency kit if she was stranded somewhere in her car. It held a sheepskin man's coat (which could be used for a blanket), a sheepskin lined cap with ear flaps, men's overalls, wool socks and mittens, a scarf, matches, flashlight, wool blanket and best of all, three Hershey chocolate bars and a bag of peanuts in the shell.

The wind was screeching so loud it took us a while to realize we had lost the radio signal. Mrs. Craig sighed and turned it off. She picked up the phone. It was dead. Not surprising, the phone lines were always the first to go. Just so the power lines didn't go down, we'd still have heat and light. I and probably everyone else was silently praying the power lines would stay standing. As long as we had heat and light we'd be just fine. The furnace burned fuel oil, but it needed electricity to spark the flame for each cycle of heat.

The older kids started making supper. If the electricity did go out we'd have at least one hot meal. Carol, Susan, Dorothy and Frank started cleaning potatoes, while Karla and Leroy started boiling eggs and filling a big kettle with water for the potatoes. Karla was actually nice, provided she was by herself.

Supper wasn't bad. We each had the rest of our lunch, plus one boiled egg and one potato with the skin on. We washed it all down with cups of hot coffee. I had never had a full cup of coffee before, just a few stolen sips from my mother's cup. It was strong and tasted terrible, but it was warm and filled me up.

I had never been in the school at night before except for the Christmas program, and that didn't really count because there were so many people there. Now, it seemed scary. Everyone went to the bathroom in the basement in small groups. The lights were so high on the ceiling there were shadows all over the place. The building moaned and groaned with the blizzard tearing at the walls. The school seemed totally cut off from the rest of the world. We could see no lights from the nearby farms or hear anything but the mournful crying of the wind.

Mrs. Craig brought out the games. Sandy, Cora, Roger, Gary and I played Pick Up Sticks. I didn't do too well because I kept bumping other sticks. It didn't help that Roger and Gary kept yelling, "Watch out!" or "Be careful." every time it was someone else's turn. After a while, we got tired of that and played Slap Jack.

Around eight o'clock, Mrs. Craig popped a big kettle of popcorn with some of the corn kernels left from Christmas. We didn't have butter, but there was salt on it. While we each munched on popcorn, she read us the story *Robinson Crusoe*. It's the story about a man who gets ship wrecked on an island. He finds a native man that he calls Friday, and they become friends. I guess, in a way, we were just as stranded as Robinson Crusoe. We would have to take care of ourselves, just as Crusoe and Friday did.

After Mrs. Craig read for a while, it was time to get ready for bed. We went to the bathroom and tried washing up with paper towels. Mrs. Craig said we should wear our snow pants, boots and hats for warmth when we slept. We would have to use our scarfs for pillows and our coats for mattresses. There were seven blankets and lots of newspaper to cover us. She suggested we sleep close together in groups for warmth.

It was weird lying on the hard floor next to Cora and Sandy. Of course, it was impossible to go to sleep, so Mrs. Craig suggested we tell stories, but no scary stories. I'm glad she said that because I was scared enough already.

Karla told about her family going west to Yellowstone Park and seeing these geysers that shot hot water out of the ground. One was called Old Faithful and at the same time every day, it would explode.

Frank said a calf was born on their farm that had two heads, but it died right away. That was kind of sad.

Of course, Andy had to share something funny. He told about the time he was on the swing and tried jumping off, but his pants were hooked on the chain. He ripped a big hole in them and had to wrap his jacket around his waist so no one could see his underwear.

Susan told about the first time she made scalloped potatoes and set the oven on five hundred degrees. The entire house filled with black smoke. It had been thirteen degrees outside, and we had every window and door open. I remembered that. We finally ended up going to Skipper's Restaurant in Merrill until the house aired out, but the smell was in the house a lot longer.

By this time, everyone was yawning and starting to feel tired. Poor exhausted Junior had fallen asleep during the stories and was lying flat on his back with his mouth open, snoring softly. Mrs. Craig flicked off the lights. The room was totally dark, with the only sound being the eerie howling of the blizzard as it whipped the snow around the building and into the windows.

I felt Cora grab my right hand and Sandy grab my left. I thought I would never sleep, because there is no way to feel comfortable on a hard wooden floor with one thin blanket and people snoring all around you, but I did.

The next morning, I woke up shivering. Cora had taken the blanket and rolled up in it. Sandy and I were entirely without a blanket. The room was lighter, but the storm was still going strong. Mrs. Craig tried the lights and they came on. Those of us awake cheered, waking up the few who were still sleeping. We were sore, stiff and still tired. My teeth and tongue felt fuzzy. I wish I had toothpaste and a toothbrush. I wish I had my parents. I wish I was home. Tears came to my eyes, but I didn't want to cry. Everyone wanted to be home and no one else was bawling, so I wiped my eyes and put on what I hoped was a big smile on my face.

"Wake up, sleepy head," I told Cora. "Breakfast is about to be served." Sandy and I pulled the blanket out of her clutching fingers.

We had a breakfast of scrambled eggs, fried potatoes and strong coffee. The older kids made the meals, and the younger kids did the cleanup.

We washed up the best we could, using toilet paper and paper towels. I don't think some of the boys even bothered, and they should have, because they were beginning to smell pretty bad.

Mrs. Craig must have thought time would go faster if we were kept busy. She had run off word searches and crossword puzzles for reading class. For arithmetic class, she had sheets for each grade level.

"How come we have to work when the other kids don't?" Karla whined from the window, where she was staring out at a wall of blowing snow.

"Shut up, Karla," Carol said. "It's easy, and I, for one, would rather be busy than staring out the window hoping the storm would stop or listening to you."

After that, no one dared complain for fear of looking like a bad sport. We knew there was no hope of going home until the storm stopped and even then it might take a day or two to get the roads plowed. The storm sure wasn't stopping yet.

Dinner was hard-boiled eggs, boiled potatoes and coffee. We each got a square of chocolate for dessert.

After eating and clean up, the entire school, including Mrs. Craig, went to the basement to play dodge ball. We were kicking up a lot of dust from the basement floor. Mrs. Craig didn't say a word. It was fun to be running and screaming.

We were in the second game, and instead of picking up the ball, Frank kicked it. It careened off the wall and through the open door of the boy's bathroom.

Leroy went to get it and yelled, "Hey, it fell down the hole!"

All the boys rushed in to see, and sure enough it had! Yuck!

We had an afternoon snack of peanuts in the shell and played board or card games. Cora and I played Cat's Cradle.

For supper, the cooks mixed together the fried potatoes and scrambled eggs. It looked pretty bad, but tasted pretty good. I'm starting to like coffee.

We played more games then had our night snack of popcorn, while Mrs. Craig read more of *Robinson Crusoe*.

There were more stories and another fitful night's sleep on the cold hard wooden floor fighting Cora for the blanket.

The next morning, I knew something was different, but at first couldn't figure out what. The storm had stopped! There was no more wailing of the wind or shaking of the windows.

I ran to the windows, where most of the kids were already standing. I couldn't believe my eyes. It was amazing! The snow was blown in soft waves against the side of the school, and the fence posts were wearing white top hats. The pine tree branches almost touched the ground from the weight of the snow and the maple and oak branches were broken off and poking out of the drifts like toothpicks. The schoolyard looked clean and white. The snow sparkled in the bright sunlight. We couldn't wait to get outside after two days of being cooped up in our little schoolhouse.

After a hurried breakfast of the last of the eggs, the usual fried potatoes and coffee, we ran screaming out into the clean freezing air. The snow was almost as high as us little kids, so we didn't do any shoveling. Mostly we threw ourselves into the drifts then went in to warm up. There were only two shovels. The older kids dug out Mrs. Craig's car and a wide enough path to the road, which was still piled high with snow. Luckily, her car started and we took turns sitting in it and listening to the radio. The announcer said that the plows were out and would get the main streets and roads first. The secondary, or least used roads, would be plowed tomorrow. Crews would be working around the clock to clear the record breaking thirty-nine inches of snow from the roads and streets. Stores and businesses were closed for two days, and everyone should stay off the roads and out of the way of the plows unless there was an emergency.

After a lunch of boiled potatoes, we were quietly sitting in groups playing board games and munching on peanuts when we heard a strange noise coming up the hill toward the school. We grabbed our coats and went outside. Led by two double snowplows, one on each side of the road, was a stream of cars and trucks blasting their horns. Every family that had kids snowed in at Tug Lake School and Mrs. Craig's husband had been plowed out and were making their way up the hill behind the plow.

The *Merrill Daily Herald*, the town newspaper, had sent a reporter and a photographer to capture the moment of our rescue. The next day, there was a big story on the front page calling Junior a hero and Mrs. Craig a resourceful teacher. There were statements from each of us about how we had felt and what we had done. Cora said that the best part of the whole thing was eating popcorn and listening to *Robinson Crusoe*. I said the worst part was missing my parents at night. There was a big picture to go along with the story. Kneeling on the floor in the front row of the picture were Sandy, Gary, Cora, me, Junior, Jake and Andy. Standing behind us were Arlene, Dorothy, Billy, Susan, Leroy, Carol, Karla, Frank and Mrs. Craig. We were a rather rag tag looking group, but the smiles were real.

Chapter Fourteen
County Spelling Bee

We didn't have school again until the following Monday. Those of us who had been stranded had a lot of sleeping and good food to catch up on. Those kids who had been delivered home safely were mad that they had missed out on all the excitement. For a few days, they treated the rest of us like movie stars.

The snowplows had cleared the ball diamond and a path up to the school for Mrs. Craig's car. The ten-foot-high snow banks gave us all kinds of new things to do at recess.

The big kids loved to play King of the Hill on the snow banks. It's fun to push and pull and drag others down the hill, but when you're one of the littler ones, you're always the one getting pushed, pulled and dragged. Even when we worked together we couldn't budge a big kid. So the littler kids found other things to do.

Cora, Sandy and I went to the far corner of the ball field and made igloos in the snow bank. We pretended they were the same the Eskimo made up by the North Pole, but of course they weren't really. We just made tunnels into a big room we made in the bank that we called our igloo. It was big enough for all three of us to sit in it. We put a hole in the roof so we could breathe. We were using chunks of snow for plates, cups and cookies. We were having a good time when Sandy suddenly exclaimed, "I don't hear anyone!"

We stopped talking and listened. There wasn't a sound from the playground. We exchanged glances and crawled out of the tunnels. The playground was deserted.

"Oh, oh!" Cora squealed. "We're going to get it now!'

We made a mad dash for the schoolhouse. It's not easy to run fast in boots, snow pants, a long wool coat, hat, scarf and mittens. Soon we were all panting and were walking as fast as possible.

By the time we had climbed to the top of the hill, our coats were unbuttoned and we had taken off our hats, scarves and mittens. The cold air felt good on our sweaty bodies.

My mother had told me never to unbutton my coat outside in winter, no matter how warm I got, because that was a good way to get a cold. My mom wasn't anywhere around, so I figured she'd never know.

We tried walking quietly to the girl's coatroom., but it's next too impossible to tip toe in six tons of winter clothes. Every eye was on us. Karla giggled. Our faces turned red, but you couldn't tell because our faces were already rosy from the cold. We hustled as fast as we could and went quickly to our seats.

Teacher didn't say one word to us, and we were never late again. The next day, we all came down with horrible colds.

The days and nights were slightly warmer. One night, a beautiful packing snow fell. The boys rolled huge snowballs and packed snow in between forming two walls about six feet away from each other. When the forts were finished, they spent the rest of the week pelting each other with snowballs every recess.

Meanwhile, the girls went to the middle of the ball diamond and started building a snow horse. We packed the snow into four blocks for legs. Next, a big flat board was laid on top of the feet for a body. Snow was packed over and around it. Then we made a head. The head wouldn't stick to the body, so we kept making it smaller and smaller. Finally, it stuck.

We stepped back to admire our work. The body was too heavy, and the head was too small. It did not look like a horse.

"It looks like a dinosaur!" Marian exclaimed.

It did. So we added a long tail that was thick near the body and thin at the end. We packed snow triangles all along its back and down its tail.

This time when we stepped away to admire it, we were proud. We named our dinosaur Horsasauris. Mrs. Craig took a picture with her Brownie box camera of all the girls standing by our creature.

As quickly as the snow came, it was gone. That's the good thing about spring snows, they don't last. With a week of temperatures in the high forties, the blizzard of the century was only a memory.

There was only a month left of school before summer vacation. It was time for the annual county spelling bee. Each school in the county would pick the two best spellers to represent their school at the district spelling championship at the Rock Falls Town Hall. For weeks, all of the fourth, fifth, sixth, seventh and eighth graders walked around with lists of spelling words, practicing. The younger grades were included, too, but when the longest word you know only has four letters, there's no way to win.

This was the only subject Susan wasn't good at. She would get A's on the Friday spelling tests then quickly forget how to spell these words the next week. I, along with everyone else, knew that Susan desperately wanted to compete at the town hall. She had never gone to the district championships before. This would be her last chance. She was in eighth grade and next year would be in high school in Merrill. Every night, Momma and Daddy would drill her with her lists of spelling words. At first, Billy helped, too. He'd give her the words, but would purposely mispronounce them. Then he'd tease her for misspelling the word. I thought she was going to throw the dictionary at him one night. After that, Billy no longer "helped," which is what he wanted in the first place.

Finally, the day of our school spelling bee came. The boys were all shoving and fooling around while the girls were twisting their hair around a finger or biting their lip.

Mrs. Craig explained the rules. She would pronounce a word, then use the word in a sentence. The speller must then say the word and spell it. No starting over or repeating of letters was accepted. If a word was misspelled, the speller would sit down at their desk and watch quietly the rest of the time. Mrs. Craig would keep repeating the word until someone spelled it correctly. The last two students standing would go to the town hall next week for the championship round.

We formed a line around the classroom. Mrs. Craig started with "baby" words, so us young kids at least got an idea of what a spelling bee was.

My first word was "if." No problem.

Gary was the first to miss a word. He spelled "when" "w-e-n."

Most of the first and second graders had sat down by the word "they." The spellers didn't seem to catch on to the fact that, if "t-h-a-y" is wrong the first time, it was still wrong the fifth time!

I missed the word "done." It's not spelled "d-u-n."

At last, there were three spellers left: Susan, Marian and Karla. Round and round the three went, spelling word after word. It was Karla's turn again. The word was "mansion." After hearing the word, Karla didn't look as smart-aleck as she had. Cora and I had our fingers crossed for Susan and Marian. Cora even had her eyes crossed. No one, except maybe Donna and Karla's cousins Frank and Jake, wanted Karla to represent our school. Karla took a big breath and let it out slowly. She spelled "m-a-n," then finished in a rush "s-h-u-n."

"No, Karla," Mrs. Craig said. "That's not correct."

She gave the word to Susan, who spelled it correctly. Everyone yelled and clapped. Marian and Susan hugged each other. Karla stomped away, grumbling that dumb old Mrs. Craig gave her the word "mansion," because Mrs. Craig wanted her favorites to win. Karla is such a poor sport.

For the next week, Susan and Marian were inseparable. When they finished their schoolwork, they would go in a quiet corner to practice spelling words with a spelling list big enough to choke an elephant. They even stayed over at each other's house to practice spelling words. Soon they were teasing each other and laughing like best friends. They had this thing going on that, if one girl said a word, the other one had to spell it correctly or they'd get a pinch. They thought that was fun! They also had some kind of private joke about the word "stretchy." Every time one of them said it, they would laugh.

The day of the district spelling bee arrived. Right after lunch, we were piled into a school bus and driven to the town hall. Even now on the bus ride over to the hall, Dorothy was quizzing Susan with a list of words in one seat and Billy was drilling Marian with a list of words in another seat. I happened to be squeezed into the same seat as Marian and Billy.

"Pneumonia," said Billy. "I thought I had pneumonia when I coughed so hard."

"That's easy," Marian answered. "My mother said to say in my mind. Silent p-neu-mon-ia, and that's how I remember it."

I wished I were in a different seat. Who cared how Marian remembered words? I wanted Susan to win.

The Rock Falls Town Hall was jammed with students and parents from five different schools in the area: Tug Lake, North Star, Woodland, Sunnyside and Rocky Hill. I saw my parents sitting near the front beside Marian's mother. They saw us and waved.

Susan and Marian gave each other a good luck hug and followed the other contestants into a side room to receive instructions. The rest of us found the section that had been saved for Tug Lake School.

The lights were dimmed except for the stage. Ten students came out in a line and turned to face the audience. They were all wearing large white circles with big black numbers on their collars. There were four boys and six girls. One girl was so short, she looked like she was in second grade.

A tall, gray-haired woman in a black suit and black high-heeled shoes came out on the stage. She spoke into a microphone that screeched so loud it hurt my ears. Someone then rushed up and fiddled with some knobs.

The woman welcomed everyone and explained the rules of the spelling bee. When she left the stage, the spelling bee began.

The woman addressed each student by their number instead of their name. Susan was called Contestant Four and Marian was Contestant Nine.

Contestant One, a tall thin girl with straggly hair and brown glasses, was given the first word, then on down the line. The spellers stood in place until it was their turn then they went up to the microphone to spell the word. Each contestant had spelled three words already, and I thought we'd be here for a month, when the boy who was Contestant Five missed the word "realize." He put an "s" instead of a "z." He was serious looking and seemed disgusted with himself. I felt sorry for him as he left the stage.

Two more contestants missed on the words "giraffe" and "poisonous."

The line on the stage got smaller until it gradually dwindled down to only four contestants: Susan, Marian. a tall boy with big ears and bushy eyebrows and the short girl who definitely wasn't in second grade.

The short girl lost on the word "bamboozle," and the boy went down shortly after, with the word "pheasant."

The only two spellers left were Susan and Marian. They smiled happily at each other, then moved closer together and hooked pinky fingers for a moment for good luck.

Susan was wearing a blue and white sailor dress and looked really pretty with her hair in a ponytail. I wished she would quit biting her bottom lip. Marian was gorgeous with her long copper-colored hair over her shoulder in a white dress with small blue flowers puffed out with can-can petticoats. The harder she concentrated, the more her freckles stood out on her nose. When it was her turn to spell, she opened and shut her hands exposing a bright pink rabbit's foot dangling from one finger. It wasn't too lucky for the rabbit.

Back and forth the words flew, both girls spelling each word correctly.

The announcer gave Marian the word "pneumonia." I wasn't paying much attention because she knew this word. I was watching a tiny spider scurry under the row of chairs in front of us when I heard everyone gasp.

"What happened?" I asked.

Dorothy leaned over my shoulder and whispered, "Marian just spelled pneumonia wrong. She missed the 'p.'"

"She couldn't have!" I exclaimed a little too loud. "She..."

"Shh!" Mrs. Craig scolded.

Susan paused a few seconds, pronounced pneumonia and spelled it correctly.

"Contestant four," said the announcer. "You are this year's championship speller for Lincoln County."

Marian gave Susan a big hug. Susan was given a big blue ribbon, a certificate saying first place and an envelope with a cash prize. Then flashbulbs started popping and everyone, including a reporter from the newspaper, rushed up on stage to congratulate and talk to Susan. Susan was shaking and crying.

Everyone had forgotten about Marian. She had been shoved to the back of the stage by the crowd surrounding Susan. Marian's mother congratulated Susan, then went over by Marian. She said one word to Marian.

"Why?"

Marian shrugged and tossed her long hair defiantly.

"This is Susan's last chance, mom. It means so much to her. I've got two more chances. I hope you're not too mad at me." Marian studied her mother's face.

Marian's mother hugged her. "I couldn't be mad at you for that, honey. We don't need a blue ribbon to know you're a winner!"

Chapter Fifteen
The End of the Year Picnic

The rainy days of April had given way to the bright sunny days of May. For three weeks we had beautiful spring weather and now tomorrow would be the school picnic and the last day of school.

Everyone was saying things like, "We'll be out of jail!" "No more stony face!" "I hate school!" I was saying these things, too, but I didn't really feel this way. Sure, I liked summer and being home, but I liked school too. I liked learning new things. I liked all the things we did at recess. I liked having a bunch of kids to play with and especially a best friend to laugh with and do things with. I'd even miss Mrs. Craig. She wasn't that bad, a little crabby and loud sometimes, but she had good ideas and read great stories like *Robinson Crusoe* and *Black Beauty*. It was lonely at home. There was no one to play with except Susan and Billy and they were always off doing their own things. I wouldn't be able to see or talk to my friends for three whole months. What if Cora found another best friend? So I felt kind of good and kind of bad about school ending.

Today was "rag and bag" day. We each had to bring a rag for cleaning and a bag to haul home all the junk we had accumulated in our desk and coatrooms. We were busy cleaning the entire school. All the floors had to be swept and scrubbed. That was the job of the eighth grade boys. Thomas and Leroy were busy slopping sudsy water all over the place from dull colored silver buckets with their string mops. Some kids were downstairs sweeping the main room and cleaning the bathrooms. It sounded more like they were playing tag rather than cleaning. Mrs. Craig sometimes raised her eyebrows when she heard a shriek or a yell, but never said anything. She had picked the kids to do the basement who were always goofing off or fooling around. I think she just wanted those kids out of the way, so everyone else could get the work done. One group was taking everything out of the kitchen cupboards and washing them and putting them back neatly. Another group was doing the same thing to the storage room. I don't think this had ever been done before, because Mrs. Craig kept running around saying, "Don't be afraid to throw things out."

Some kids were up on ladders and tables washing windows and wiping down spider webs. It was like spring cleaning at home except we were getting ready to close school for three months.

John, Roger, Gary, Sandy, Cora and I were responsible for covering the library shelves with newspaper to keep the dust out. Anyway, most of us were busy taping the paper over the shelves. Roger was running around singing:

> *"School's out, school's out*
> *Teacher let the fools out!*
> *Some went east*
> *Some went west*
> *Some hid under the teacher's desk."*

After about twenty minutes of this singing, Junior, who was on a ladder washing windows, threw his sponge at Roger. It just missed him and hit Mrs. Craig in the shoulder. She picked it up, gave him a stern look and playfully hit Junior right in the chest with the sponge.

Carol came running over to me. "Here's your missing mitten," she said, handing me a striped mitten that had gone missing in January.

"Where was it?"

"It was pushed way in the back on the shelf in the boys' coatroom. How did it get there?" Carol asked.

I shrugged, having no idea.

When the cleaning was finished, it was time for lunch. On nice days, Cora, Sandy and I ate our lunches on the merry-go-round. We'd sit on the edge eating our sandwiches and swinging our feet as it gently turned. We had to eat fast because kids would want to play here. It's hard to eat a sandwich while twirling in a circle. We've tried!

After eating, the three of us played hopscotch in the sand of the outfield of the ball field. I didn't have my hopscotch rock, so I used the mitten Carol had found. I won. Cora said that I had cheated because a mitten is easier to pick up than a rock. She's right, but I didn't mean to cheat.

After dinner, we cleaned our desks. That meant taking everything out, putting the textbooks in the big metal cabinet in the supply room, taking home all your things and washing the desk inside and out and drying it. I wonder where all the little stuff comes from that hides under the books and notebooks. John had not taken one school paper home all year. He had been saving them. That probably explains why the lid of his desk never closed! His brother, Thomas, helped him stuff all of his papers in brown paper bags. He filled up four of them! Gary really had to scrub to get the pencil drawings off his desk and Andy spent a long time scraping dried up bubble gum off the bottom of his desk. Then we shoved all the desks to one side of the room and set up the folding chairs for the eighth grade graduation.

* * *

Picnic day was warm and sunny. We practiced for the graduation. Then we took the tables outside for the picnic and set up folding chairs around the tables for our parents and families. The kids would sit and eat on the grass or wherever they wanted to. Mrs. Craig had a big pile of paper plates and plastic forks. Two big metal wash tubs were set in the shade and big blocks of ice were laid over the pop bottles in the bottom of the tub. When it was time for the picnic, the ice would be melted and the pop would be cold.

Since it was picnic day, we were allowed to wear home clothes to school, not the usual dresses for girls and dress shirts and pants for the boys. The girls wore dungarees and bobby socks. The boys wore jeans and old shirts. Since it probably was all right if we got a little dirty, we chose teams for an all school softball game. Mrs. Craig would be the umpire. I can't hit, throw, or catch very well, so I was one of the last ones picked. Cora and Sandy didn't do much better. Sandy and I ended up on the same team.

Our team was out in the field first. Junior played first base. Susan was second base and Diane played third. Frank was the catcher. The rest of us were spread out in the field. Sandy and I were way, way out by the fence where we hoped no one could hit the ball. The team wanted Arlene as the pitcher, but Karla grabbed the ball and marched to the pitcher's mound. She was a lousy pitcher. After the third inning we were down by eight runs.

"Karla, get out of there!" Frank shouted. "You can't pitch yourself out of a brown paper bag!"

"Shut up!" she yelled back to her cousin. "It's not my fault no one is catching anything in the air."

"They're never in the air," Frank retorted. "You're walking everyone. You can't even strike out the little kids."

That didn't stop Karla from pitching. It just made her mad, and her pitches became even wilder. She was throwing as hard as she could and finally got a pitch into the strike zone. The only problem was that the bases were loaded and Ned (their best hitter) was up to bat. He swung as hard as he could. I could hear the crack of the bat as it connected with the ball. The speeding ball was headed right for Karla and plowed right into her stomach. Karla was knocked right onto her back. She lay there gasping for breath as the ball rolled unnoticed over the grass. Four runs scored and still our team didn't move. Mrs. Craig headed for the pitcher's mound where Karla lay gasping like a fish out of water and rapidly blinking her eyes. Donna beat Mrs. Craig to the mound.

"Are you all right?" Donna squeaked nervously.

"Oh, shut up," Karla snarled as she scrambled to her feet. "Here," she picked up the forgotten ball and tossed it to Arlene. "You want to pitch so bad, go ahead."

When everyone realized that Karla wasn't permanently injured and was her old lovable self, everyone started laughing. I laughed so hard my stomach ached. Leroy and Junior had tears rolling down their cheeks. Just when things settled down, Andy flung himself on the ground and did an imitation of Karla opening and shutting her mouth and blinking her eyes. That started everyone hooting and hollering again. Karla grabbed Donna by the arm and huffed off the field. She looked at Marian, but she was busy laughing with Billy. I guess maybe that was what Billy had meant that first day of school when he said Karla would get hers. She sure did, right in the stomach! Actually, she had gotten it twice. Once now and once when the tree fell on her. I guess it doesn't pay to be mean.

The parents started arriving with their cars and pickups loaded with food and little kids. Now I understood why Mrs. Craig set the tables outside. She didn't want her clean school all messed up again. The tables were loaded with a lot of food. I hoped they wouldn't break. There were ground baloney and egg salad sandwiches, potato salads, macaroni salads, Jell-O salads, fruit salads, pickles, cucumbers, beets, cow's tongue and my favorite, pickled crab-apples, baked beans, cold slaw. Plus, there were all kinds of desserts; all kinds of cookies, cupcakes in two favors, several pans of brownies and five huge watermelons.

Everyone was milling around talking while cars were still arriving, when suddenly Jimmy's mother screamed.

"My baby, my baby!"

Jimmy's little brother, Ricky, was running just as fast as his little chubby two-year-old legs could help him down the hill right into the path of a car that was pulling into the school yard. Jimmy's mother started running but she was too far away and heavy to get to him in time. I was so scared that I couldn't stand to watch. I opened my eyes when I heard the sound of clapping. There was Roger grinning from ear to ear holding a struggling and screaming Ricky, who was very much alive!

Roger had been down by the cars greeting his foster parents when he saw Ricky running straight for the oncoming car. He had scooped up the baby and kept running, with no thought to his own safety. Jimmy's mother took her little boy from Roger's arms and held him tight to her chest. Ricky didn't like this either, and kept screaming and struggling until she sat him down with a peanut butter cookie at her feet. Everyone was slapping Roger on the back and telling him what a brave thing he had done.

After things had settled down a little, Mrs. Craig presented Roger with a hastily made blue ribbon that said "Hero." She pinned it on his shirt.

We had two wonderful surprises.

Mrs. Webb came with her little baby girl, Sharon Rose. Mrs. Webb remembered everyone's name and let the big girls hold the baby. Sharon had a round, chubby face like her mother. She was bald and blue-eyed with the tiniest fingers and toes I had ever seen. She was wearing a frilly pink dress with matching bonnet and little booties that she kept kicking off. Sharon was a happy child and was smiling and chortling at everyone as they played pass the baby.

I could hardly believe my eyes when I saw the next surprise. Judy was being carried up the hill by her dad. He set her down at the top of the hill and she walked the last few steps by herself. She was wearing the heavy shoes with braces and using crutches, but she was slowly and proudly walking toward the tables.

The entire Tug Lake School, students, families and friends, rushed over by Judy. There were a million questions and everyone was talking at once trying to get Judy's attention.

"How are you?"

"Can you stay home for good, or are you just visiting?"

"You're really looking good!"

"Do you need any help?"

Judy was concentrating on negotiating the uneven ground. She didn't say anything, but she looked pleased at seeing all her friends and proud to be walking on her own. It must have taken a lot of work for her to walk so well in only a few months.

When Judy reached the tables, everyone applauded. Andy brought up a chair and Judy explained that she was only visiting. She told how Mrs. Craig had gotten special permission so she could go home for a few days and attend the graduation. Mrs. Craig seemed slightly embarrassed at the mention of that. I'm beginning to think that Mrs. Craig is not as grumpy as she tries to make people think she is.

It took a long time for everyone to settle down and start to eat, but when we got started, we couldn't stop. Everyone went back for seconds, thirds and even fourths of the good food, while of course visiting with Mrs. Webb and Judy and each other. It was good to see Judy holding Mrs. Webb's little girl. Sharon would grab handfuls of Judy's hair, and Judy would laugh as she untangled the little hands.

At the meal, Ricky's mom made Roger sit right by her and kept his plate filled. She kept hugging him, pinching his cheek and calling him her "little hero," while making sure Ricky was never two steps away from her. Even Mrs. Craig gave Roger the largest slice of watermelon. I didn't know such a skinny kid could hold so much food! For the rest of the day, everyone made a big fuss over him.

It was getting close to chore time, so finally everyone went inside for the eighth grade graduation. I was so full, I could hardly move, let alone sing. I think everyone felt the same way because the song *America* started off pretty draggy, but by the time we got to the part where Lois and Roger sang together, with the rest of us humming in the background, it sounded pretty good.

The eighth graders had changed into dress clothes. Thomas and Leroy were in suits and ties, looking mighty uncomfortable. Carol had a blue dress with white lace trim, and Susan was wearing a white dress with a wide pink satin ribbon around her waist. Arlene had a pretty green dress with a full skirt, and Dorothy's red dress looked great with her dark hair.

First, the eighth graders read their last wills and testaments.

Thomas left his desk to his little brother, John, so that John would have more room to store his papers next year.

Carol left her hook in the coatroom to me, so I wouldn't get pinned behind the door anymore.

Leroy left his job as softball pitcher to Karla because he knew she wanted it. Everyone but Karla laughed at that.

Dorothy left her arithmetic book to Junior because some of the answers were penciled in and she knew he'd like that.

Susan said that she would have left her blue spelling ribbon to Marian, but she knew Marian would get her own next year. Marian blushed, but she looked mighty pleased. Then Susan said she would leave her ability to get straight "A's" to Billy and me. She can give it to Billy because he doesn't do his homework, but I can earn my own "A's," thank you very much.

Arlene was going to leave her back seat in the bus to Frank, who was always trying to beat her to it. Frank stood up and raised his hands like a prize fighter. Everyone laughed.

Because Susan had the best grades in her class, she had the honor of giving a little speech. Most of it was boring, and I spent the time watching little Ricky blow bubbles with his spit as he slept in his mother's arms.

Then Susan started mentioning some of the things she remembered from her eight years at Tug Lake School. I started thinking back to all the fun, exciting and scary things that happened in my first year of school. I looked around the room at my friends. There was Roger sitting proudly with his blue hero ribbon pinned to his shirt, and Judy with her crutches propped up by her chair. Andy was acting like an ape to make Mrs. Webb's baby laugh and my best friend Cora was wrapping her hair ribbon around her leg. What a busy year this had been, and best of all, I could read! I could hardly wait for the next seven years at Tug Lake School.

Games Played at Tug Lake School

Batter's Up

Billy loved playing Batter's Up because he was really good at it. The batter tosses the softball into the air and hits it with the bat to the kids standing in the field. If a kid catches it in the air on the fly, you get a turn to go up and bat. If the kid traps it on the ground, they get ten points. The first one to one hundred gets to bat next.

Marbles

There are many ways to play marbles. This is the simple way it was played at Tug Lake by the younger boys. There was a round circle worn in the dirt at the back of the schoolhouse. Depending on how many were playing, the boys put in from one to five marbles. Someone who wasn't playing, prepared blades of grass and held them so the boys could pick. Long blade went first, etc. Then they'd use a big marble called a shooter and shoot from the shooter line. Any of the marbles they got out of the circle, they keep. If they miss or the shooter stays in the circle their turn is over. The kid who ended up with the most marbles was the winner. Cora, Sandy, and I tried marbles a few times but we didn't like getting dirt under our fingernails.

Around the World

This is a game played with math facts flash cards. One student would stand up by another student's desk. The teacher would flash a card. The first student to answer correctly would move to the next desk. The loser would sit down at that desk. When someone had gotten back to their own desk, they had gone around the world. Once Ned came, it wasn't as much fun because he could go around the world without sitting down.

Jump Rope

Most of the girls loved to play jump rope every recess, except the older girls who just stood around and talked about boys or Eddie Fisher and Elizabeth Taylor. We didn't use real rope. Our jump ropes were made from binder twine. Binder twine is a strong string used to tie up hay bales. We'd use several strings of binder twine and braid it to make it heavy enough to use as a jump rope. I was one of the best jump ropers in the school. My favorite jump rope rhyme was Teddy Bear because you got to do fun things like touch the ground, pretend to tie your shoe and run out of the jump rope without tripping.

Teddy bear, teddy bear
Turn around
Teddy bear, teddy bear
Touch the ground
Teddy bear, teddy bear
Tie your shoes
Teddy bear, teddy bear
Out goes you.

Auntie-I-Over

Choose two teams. One team on each side of the building. We just played over the new entrance because it would take too long to run around the entire school. The team with the ball would throw it over the roof and yell Auntie-I-Over. If a team caught it, they would run around the building and try to hit members of the other team to take them back to their side. If they didn't catch the ball, they would throw it back over the roof. When one side has all the players the game is over. Don't play in the winter the ball is hard and leaves bruises.

Fox and Geese

This game is best played in fresh snow. A leader tramps a big circle in the snow and everyone follows stamping down the snow. Then make a trail north and south in the circle and one east and west. Now there are four sections. Where the points meet is the goal. "It" is the fox and the rest are geese. When It catches someone they are the new It. Don't cross the sections, you'll get yelled at.

Card Games

A couple of our favorite card games were Slap Jack and Old Maid.

Slap Jack

Deal an even number of cards to each player. Each person takes turns laying down one card at a time. If a Jack shows up, slap it and you get the cards in the pile. The first one to get all the cards is the winner.

Old Maid

We used regular playing cards with the Queen of Clubs being the Old Maid. Then you draw cards from each other, putting down the matches until someone is stuck with the Old Maid. Don't play with Cora, she cheats.

Jacks

In the game of Jacks there are ten little metal stars called jacks and a small ball. The jack player throws the jacks onto the ground, making sure none are touching, and tosses the little ball into the air. The idea is to pick up a jack and catch the ball on the first bounce, all with the same hand. When a player has successfully picked up all the jacks in one turn, they have to pick up two jacks at a time, called twosies, then threesies, and so forth. The highest I've managed to go is fivesies, but Cora has been through tensies and started "moonsies"; where you make a circle around the ball, pick up the jack and catch the ball, all before the ball bounces twice.

Bird, Beast or Fish

Let's say I am It. I point to Fred and yell beast. Then I start counting to ten. One, two, three, four... If Fred would say bear before I'm done counting, I'm still It. If he doesn't answer correctly, he's It and no repeating of names. I wish Cora would learn that just because there is a catfish, doesn't mean there is a cowfish!

Cat's Cradle

One person holds a loop of string around both their hands. Another person picks up the string in two places, crossing it. This continues until the string looks like a tangled spider web. Then one person picks the right two spots and the string is just one loop again.

Pick Up Sticks

In the game of pick up sticks there are thirty-one colored wooden sticks that look like long toothpicks with two pointy ends. You throw the sticks down. Then the idea is to pick up one stick at a time without moving the others. If you move any stick but the one you are picking up; your turn is over. When the sticks are all picked, everyone adds their points. There are six sticks each of red, blue, yellow, green, and orange. Yellow sticks are five points. Green and orange is ten, and red and blue is twenty. The black stick is fifty points. Be careful or you'll poke out an eye!

Kick the Can

We had a big Folgers coffee can we turned over and used for a goal. One person was it. The rest of the kids ran around the school building and hid. It would have to go find them and run back to the can; put one foot on the can and count one, two, three on Jimmy, one, two, three on Carol and anyone else they saw. If someone beat you back to the can, they would kick it and free everybody and It would have to start over.

King of the Hill

Of course, this was only played in winter. Everyone would try to scramble to the top of the hill while others were trying to stop them by pulling them down. Be careful that you don't rip someone's coat. One time Dorothy had her boot pulled off and was really mad cause Tommy filled it with snow before he gave it back because he really likes her. Boys are so strange. Don't hang on to wire fences because you can pull a section down. Then when the snow melts in the spring the cows get out and leave cow-pies all over the school yard.

Dodge Ball

We played dodge ball by half the kids making a circle and the other half going in the middle of the circle. The kids on the outside throw the ball and try to hit the kids in the circle waist down, if it was above the waist it didn't count. If you were hit you join the circle. Don't kick the ball.

Hopscotch

Draw ten rectangles on the ground in a pattern. Throw your rock on a rectangle. For example: If it lands in number eight, you have to hop on one or two feet, depending on the pattern and pick it up without falling Sandy, Cora, and I keep track by drawing lines in the sand for each turn. When recess is over we count them up.

Made in the USA
Lexington, KY
05 December 2016